SLEEP TIGHT
SATELLITE

SLEEP TIGHT SATELLITE

BY CAROL GUESS

TUPELO PRESS
NORTH ADAMS, MASSACHUSETTS

Sleep Tight Satellite
Copyright © 2023 Carol Guess.

ISBN 978-1-946482-90-7 (paperback)

Library of Congress Control Number: 2023005290

Cover and text designed by Kenji Liu.

Cover art by Sarah Salcedo, courtesy of Tall Firs Productions.

First paperback edition October 2023

Tupelo Press
P.O. Box 1767
North Adams, Massachusetts 01247
(413) 664-9611 / Fax: (413) 664-9711
editor@tupelopress.org / www.tupelopress.org

Tupelo Press is an award-winning independent literary press that publishes fine fiction, non-fiction, and poetry in books that are a joy to hold as well as read. Tupelo Press is a registered 501(c)(3) non-profit organization, and we rely on public support to carry out our mission of publishing extraordinary work that may be outside the realm of the large commercial publishers. Financial donations are welcome and are tax deductible.

"The Music Dance Experience is officially canceled."

MILCHICK, *SEVERANCE*

TABLE OF CONTENTS

ACKNOWLEDGMENTS

"Alternative Teaching Modalities in Hell"—*McSweeney's Internet Tendency*

"Epistemology"—*Tampa Review*

"Memorandum of Understanding Regarding Replacements Should the Worst Outcome Occur"—*McSweeney's Internet Tendency*

"Mock City" (as "Gun Safe")—*STAT®REC*

"Or"—*The Georgia Review*

"Q&A" (as "Cuttings")—*"Journal of Compressed Creative Arts*

"Sleep Tight Satellite"—*Tupelo Quarterly*

"The Next Story"—*Tupelo Quarterly*

✳

Cover art by Sarah Salcedo, courtesy of Tall Firs Productions.

✳

Thanks to my friends and family, especially Dillon Kreider, Meg Brown, Nichola Torbett, Leslie Scott, Harvey Hawks, Jeanne Yeasting, and Debra Salazar.

Thanks to Kristina Marie Darling, Jeffrey Levine, David Rossitter, and all at Tupelo Press; to Sarah Salcedo for the cover art; to my colleagues and students at Western Washington University; and to Rochelle Hurt, Rachel Corwin, Ted Zee, Aimee Parkison, Suzanne Paola, Bruce Beasley, Robert Lashley, Wendy Fox, Alison Bruns, Jane Blunschi, Hillary Leftwich, Kelly Weber, Kristy Bowen, Lee Banner, Kier Schumaker, Star Rush, chip phillips, and my poem-a-day friends for creating community.

This book is dedicated with love to my mother, Gerry.

ONE

MOCK CITY

Every Monday, Mock City. You get up at five am, but instead of driving north to the airport, you drive south through strip malls and suburbs. You drive to the police academy where you were trained and now work one morning a week. Mock City interrupts the parking lot of the academy, a rectangular building with vinyl siding, handwritten signage, and too many doors. It's the same script every Monday, fake rooms with fake furniture. The police recruits change, but they read the same lines. You guide them through mock scenes, composites of real cases: a bar fight with broken bottles, someone's suicidal spouse locked in their bedroom, a domestic violence call where three people answer, all narrating at once. Social workers roleplay civilians. The social workers are in training for dealing with you.

The rest of the week you work at the airport, a maze of detours, circular gates. It's rote until it's not. It's following the rules until someone doesn't. It's the same and the same until something explodes. At the airport you sit in an office high above the food court, overlooking pretzels and cocktails, greasy pizza to go. You're invisible behind one-way glass, guns at the ready in rooms filled with family photos and instant coffee. The view from your office window is an advertisement shaped like a suitcase, seams leaking smoke spelling *Report Unattended Luggage!*

"Was that your idea?"

"Do I look like Marketing?"

You're wearing your uniform, bulletproof vest, gun, Taser, latex gloves, badge, and American flag pin.

You do not look like Marketing.

∗

You're in roll call and then you're at your desk and suddenly you're racing through the airport to stop the guy with the hunting rifle staring down some anxious underpaid TSA agent.

You're in roll call and then you're at your desk and suddenly the country explodes, spontaneous demonstrations at airports nationwide, protesting the travel ban.

"See you on the other side of the barricades!"

You don't laugh. And later: "Don't kiss me when I'm in uniform."

"Don't kiss me when I'm gossiping at the water cooler."

You don't laugh and then we're sleeping. Your gun is in the safe, but you won't teach me about gun safety because why would I ever touch your gun?

"But what if some guy breaks in and you reach for it, but he shoots you first and it's just me and you're dead and you can't reach your gun?"

"If I'm dead and I can reach my gun, you're really in trouble."

I don't laugh and then we're sleeping. Your gun is in the safe and you say it's safer this way, safer that I'll never know how it works.

※

We watch a Scandinavian crime drama on TV. You point out every wrong thing the heroine does. She runs wrong, she points the gun wrong, she cuffs the suspect wrong, she cuffs the wrong suspect. She speaks Swedish and has long pale hair and watery blue eyes like mine.

Your eyes are also watery blue. Your skin is even paler than mine. You kiss me. We make out but don't have sex because sex is sometimes too upsetting to you. My noises, you say, sound violent. In the beginning, I wanted sex so badly I'd stroke you through your pants while we were eating dinner, but you pushed my hand away so I just stopped.

Once every two weeks you climb on top of me and grunt and the noises echo in the room. We both come quickly. If I don't come, you put your tongue on me and then I do but it's all over in a couple of minutes.

While we're fucking sometimes I think about Mock City. I imagine a scene where no one gets caught, two happy people, no broken glass. They're lying in bed, no blood stain, no weapon. They're kissing, slapping, licking, and thrusting. They last a long time, but we're done just like that.

※

My best friend chokes on her coffee. "A gun? Why would someone leave a gun at your house?"

"Not gun, gun safe."

"It has a gun in it, yes?"

"The gun goes with the person; it's the safe that stays."

※

When you walk through the door, gun under your shirt, I reach for you in my hungry way but it unnerves you, as if I might steal your gun. I learn to stand very still while you remove the bullets, while you unlock the safe, while you lock it all down.

Sometimes I watch you, looking for clues to the part of you that knows how to kill. When you kiss me all I feel is your mouth, but sometimes your hand tickles my throat.

✳

One of the cops on your shift at the airport goes through a bad breakup, the kind where X leaves stuff on Y's doorstep. You describe her opening the door, seeing the black metal box on her porch, dropped as if from a plane, every word recorded, every kiss, every song, every fuck, every fight.

"You know it's over when your girlfriend gives you back your gun safe."

I don't laugh and then we're sleeping. Your gun is in the safe, the safe is in the closet, the closet is in the bedroom, the bedroom is in my house.

✳

Halfway through airport security I feel someone watching. The police dog sniffs my bag as I pull my belt out of my jeans.

"Do we still take out our laptops?" No one seems to know. The guy in front of me texts furiously and the pair bond behind me melds into a clingy mass of inflatable neck pillows.

"Does mace count as explosives?" No one seems to know this, either.

"Yes and yes."

I look up and it's you. You're on duty; I'd forgotten, but had I really? Had I really forgotten, or had I planned my entire trip to see my maybe dying uncle to coordinate with your beat circling the airport, you and your Kevlar, your tactical aim?

I'm so well-trained not to kiss you that I think *Don't shoot!* as if you're a cop with a loaded gun.

✳

One day I'm washing dishes, my back turned toward you, and I ask about the thing I see, the way you recoil sometimes during sex, your hesitation, your closed eyes, your detachment.

I say I see you. I say I see how it is. I say you can talk to me. I say you can tell me anything. I say I don't want it to be like that for you anymore. I say you shouldn't ever do anything you don't want to do, not for anyone. I say I love you. I say …

The door slams.

You come home an hour later.

"I have something to show you," you say, holding your phone horizontally. When you tap the screen, it's baby goats in pajamas. The littlest one keeps getting kicked in the head.

✳

Our day arrives, and you show me Mock City.

The building looks exactly as you described it. Recruits cluster outside, away from the doors. You explain that standing away from doors becomes second nature.

"Anything can come out of a door."

We walk inside. I'm proud to be with you, but also know I'm not the first and probably won't be the last. The other officers have seen this before, small blonde beta trailing behind.

You push open the door and I follow you. It smells like gym, sweat socks, and blood. The concrete walls glare dirty white. Every room has windows opening onto the corridor, handwritten signs marking each scene: *DV, Suicide, Dementia, Mental Health.*

"It should say *Mental Illness*. The sign says *Health*."

You look at me like I'm crazy, the same look you give me when I talk about my friends, friends who padlock themselves to fences, who grow roots in asphalt while the president plays golf.

You show me the fake jail cell first: cot with soiled blanket, bloodstains on the wall. Then a fake airport terminal and a fake bus station with real busses. For a time, you're leading scenes in the barroom brawl. I watch the same play over and over, actors fumbling unrehearsed lines. Once in a while someone sparks, grabs the social worker, wrestles away the knife. Once in a while someone says the right thing, tough but with a hint of compassion, because we're all in it together, and what we're all in is danger. But mostly it's rote, distracted, balloons floating above the room, and the actors acting their hearts out for me.

Everyone breaks for lunch. Someone brings coffee on a cardboard tray, someone brings sandwiches. Everyone jokes about beer. One of your buddies takes out his laser pointer and shoots you in the chest, red dot to heart. You fall on the floor, mock dead. Everyone laughs and then you're eating, bits of lettuce falling to the floor of the fake bar, Top Forty blasting through real speakers.

After lunch, more scenes, then a buzzer goes off and everyone stops mid-sentence. The suicidal social worker laughs and checks his phone; the robber social worker drops the purse; the elderly social worker is still elderly and asks for her check. You gesture toward the door and we're back in the hall, heading toward the exit, where I'll ask too many questions and your face will stay closed.

But we don't take the door leading outside. Instead, when the corridor is empty, you push me up against the dirty wall and kiss me. Then you give me a look as if to say, "Now."

You walk away from the exit, into the deep. The building goes on and on, stairs leading up, stairs leading down. We walk and walk, more stairs, more down, landings that open onto hallways of doors. Sometimes we pass someone who glances at you and you gesture toward me, signaling something I can't decipher. We walk until finally the corridor stops.

We are in a corridor and there are two doors. You stand in front of the doors and I wait for you to tell me which door to open. But you don't say anything. Since you aren't talking, I pick. Both doors have windows the size of TV screens. I peer through the window of the door on the right, expecting it to look like the others. But this room is different. Inside, through the screen, the scene looks real. It looks realer than real. There's a road, light fading, toward evening, and the road has a double yellow line and there are two cars pulled over to the side. One of the cars has flashing lights. A cop gets out of the car and walks toward the other car, which is grey and dented and old. The cop looks in the window of the car. Raps on the glass. Just then I feel you turn away from the window, but it's too late; I can't not look. I can't stop seeing the cop step back, gesturing for the driver to get out of the car. The driver holds up his hands and for a second, I think the scene is over. It was practice, a practice traffic stop. This is how you do it. This is how you stop someone for speeding, fine them, write them a ticket, tell them to slow down.

Instead the cop knees the man, pushes him to the ground. The man falls to the road and light from a hotel blinks on and off in the trees. The man doesn't have a gun, doesn't have anything.

He's saying stop.

He's saying don't shoot.

The cop leans back, then steps forward and kicks the man. Kicks him again, in the chest, in the head. The cop takes aim as the man begs with bloody mouth: Stop! Don't shoot!

Moonlight burns the trees.

Gunshots shatter the silence between us.

I'm heaving, sick. I bend over in the corridor and throw up, everything out of my body, wanting out of my skin.

I turn around because I need you to comfort me. Tell me everything will be okay. Tell me about actors, how they're paid in Mock City, how at the end of the day everyone goes out for drinks.

But when I turn around, you're gone. The road stretches for miles. It's evening. I'm stopped by the side of the road.

SLEEP TIGHT SATELLITE

When the pandemic hit, I drove out of Seattle. I knew a guy who owed me a favor. He let me use his winter place, a cabin for all the things he did in snow.

I told a few friends I was leaving, put my dog in the front seat and a suitcase in the back. When I stopped for gas in Everett I felt like an extra in a zombie movie. The freeway was mostly empty, a few cars driving too fast or too slow, headlights piercing water-logged farmland. Nothing was open except gas stations, automated card readers still counting gallons. I got a can of soda from a vending machine and peed in the shrubbery beside a ball field. On the radio, announcers exhaled static, cutting news with upbeat music and pre-recorded interviews from The Before Times.

It took about three hours to get from Seattle to Alger. When I showed up at the cabin, the woods were dark, a thick velvety feeling weighed down at the edges. The key was hidden under a lawn ornament by the back door. A plastic deer, big weepy eyes. Inside was more what I'd expected, everything creamy white with dark gray accents, live edge wood furniture, a few throw pillows in muted blues. The kitchen gleamed silver, white subway tile on the backsplash. It was glossy and completely unrelated to the environment, to the greens and browns outside the door. Like my guy had picked up a condo on Capitol Hill and moved it to the woods. I wasn't complaining. Not a bad place to live or die, whichever way this was going. I texted photos to friends as if beauty had brought me and might tempt me to stay.

I knew I wouldn't go back to the city. This wasn't a vacation, a getaway. This was the start of the collapse. There would be no end to this. The President was burning the country to the ground and the sense that anyone might die at any time stopped being an existential theory and became urgent reality. I figured I was lucky. My building was eight stories high, on a busy city street, surrounded by taller buildings, people moving in and out, touching things, exhaling steam. Surely this would be safer. I wouldn't have to wipe the door handles, change my clothes every time I went in and out, make small talk that might kill me. If I got it, if I breathed glass, if my feet turned red and my eyes rimmed pink and my head split and I didn't have the energy to stand up, well, then. I had friends who expected a text every three days. If four days went by, they'd come get the dog.

"Stay as long as you'd like," my guy said. He was in Canada, safe side of the border. He had a house in Victoria, a flat in Vancouver. He was in a pandemic pod with two attractive strangers, each meeting different sexual proclivities and duties on a chore wheel. He had dual citizenship and wasn't setting foot in the infection zone. When I asked if I could join the trio, his voice trailed off. Besides, they'd closed the border, Americans shut out from all the countries the President had insulted. I couldn't cross over to Canada even if his pandemic pod voted me in. That was when he offered me his cabin.

"It's close to Lake Whatcom but it feels like the middle of nowhere. Just don't feed the deer," he said. "They carry diseases."

In April I was optimistic for about three days. Then the weight of knowing descended, fog that rolled across the lake. I understood that survival wasn't just about not getting the virus. I needed to stay sane. I needed rituals, patterns I could follow. I needed a sense of structure.

Every day I cut something. A strand of hair, a fingernail, a fallen leaf in half at the ribs. I chopped wood. I cut potatoes from a sack I'd brought with me, dropped pale cubes into canned soup. Every day I walked the dog in figure eights up rural roads, through woods at the end of the last closed loop. Every day I worked, typing words and strings of numbers into my laptop.

Work was the one thing that stayed exactly the same. My job had always been work from home. We were over it by now: the accidental bathroom shots, the slips where someone's naked lap flashed onscreen. We were over how it turned everyone into workaholics, how surveillance never stopped, how the absence of a commute simply translated into more time onscreen. How people answered messages at 3am expecting a reply. Getting a reply. Getting up, rolling over to the other side of the bed and calling it a desk. Honestly, it was a relief that suddenly the entire country was as miserable and burnt out as we were.

My job was mechanical engineering, specifically satellites. My job was making top secret fuel-filled silver stars that snapped photographs, stories people wanted outer space to tell. Everything piecemeal, compartmentalized. No one person had the big picture. The only big picture was the satellite's eye. We knew what we were doing was sometimes good and sometimes wrong, but none of that was supposed to matter. We were simply the satellite's handlers. If what we handled was unethical, how would we ever know if all we saw was a piece of the puzzle, the raw red edge of a frozen frame?

All along the afternoon my neighbors' kids flew kites on the banks of Lake Whatcom. Raced the hilly roads in wheelbarrows. On my walks in the woods everything fit together, fern fronds etching dirt pocked with deer scat. I rescued beetles overturned on gravel roads. Once, I saw a slug prickly with pine needles like a porcupine. I wondered if the needles hurt. While I watched, the slug slothed across the road to get to the other side, brown needles swaying as its long green body lugged the extra weight onward.

On another walk, I found a wooden arrow resting in a pile of leaves like sleep. The arrow was the first thing that scared me. The second was a gray-haired woman I never saw again calling to me from her front porch, "You look out for the cougar, now. She's got her cubs. It's not safe to be walking the way you do." A small tenderness, her worry, but my world was so small already. Still, I found a ski pole and began carrying it on walks with the dog.

My days were lonely. Work expanded into moonlit hours that used to be mine. I thought of The Before Times, how I sat with my wife, touching her thigh, sliding my hand beneath her skirt until it felt so easy to raise her skirt and kneel, to put my mouth on her. How we couldn't marry until suddenly the state rolled us over, made our domestic partnership a marriage by that time we didn't want. She loved someone else. She thought I loved my satellites too much. Maybe I did. Now I loved slugs ferrying a forest of needles, soft deer riddled with ticks, a pile of pierced leaves.

✳

Days slipped into weeks into months and I lost track of the calendar. My entire work life was now asynchronous, which meant that I worked seven days a week from morning to night and dreamed of shiny objects orbiting earth in outer space. My friends and I talked on the phone, and all our love for each other was there, but we had nothing to look forward to until the next call. My satellites provided a sense of adventure. I was working on Suomi NPP, imaging weather, a code I was born to decipher. Wind, rain, snow, floods, hurricanes, tornados spoke to outer space and outer space spoke back. When I closed my eyes, I saw the photographs we'd taken as if I was floating above my apocalyptic planet.

The call came in July. I knew it was July because the woods filled with fireworks. Setting fire to exploding sticks in a dry summer forest seemed unwise, especially with signs reading *Burn Ban In Effect* all along the roads leading to town. But one night the sky exploded, and my phone, when I checked, confirmed it was the Fourth. Burning sticks in a tinderbox, the country divided against itself. A few days later, the phone rang. No one ever called from work, so I thought it was a candidate asking for money. But when I answered, I recognized the voice: my boss. For a second I was scared I'd been fired.

I would no longer be working on Suomi, they said. Not because I hadn't done a good job. My job, they said, had been too good. I was needed, they said, elsewhere. I would be contacted to begin high security clearance. If I had anything in my past that might need explaining, I should speak up now.

I said nothing.

The call ended with a click.

How do you mourn weather, its elegant math? I had images burned into my retina from working on the weather satellite. I was used to looking down, seeing the swirl of life on the planet below. What happened to my human body felt inconsequential compared to my spinning globe.

What would I work on now? What shiny flying object would I grow to love? My ex-wife was wrong; I didn't love satellites more than I loved her. I just loved humans and objects differently. I loved waking up to her leg thrown carelessly over my leg. I loved her patterns, her routines. I loved the shape her mouth made when she was just about to speak and her gaze when she listened, taking something in. It was me she didn't love. I was the eccentricity of an elliptical orbit. I was the outlier she couldn't control.

The woman she left me for was loud, filled rooms with little imagination and endless jokes. Was predictable. They were clumsy and human together. Smoked too much pot and watched reality TV. What I missed about my wife was what we'd made together, a collaboration. But because we each saw only our orbit, the universe from our small point of view, we'd lost the big picture. I wondered if she sometimes thought of me. If she missed me. I invented great silver birds that flew. Secretly I named each satellite for her.

Now I was losing Suomi. Whatever they were moving me to would mean staring at a tiny corner of something I'd never understand. I'd get a raise, but my grasp of the world would dissolve. From here on out, everything would be abstract. I might not be working on satellites at all.

I passed the initial security clearance. In stages, they said. Be ready for a knock on your door. I wasn't worried; there was the gay thing, but that wasn't a secret these days. The company even had a networking group. I'd gone to a few lunches, a few talks in The Before Times, mostly to see who else was queer. But the group's impulse was always to do queer things—softball games, a Pride float. I just wanted to feel safe at work. I just didn't want to get fired because I had a wife instead of a husband, because I refused to wear heels or defer to men.

I did have secrets, but so did everyone. The security clearance process was only interested in particular secrets. I didn't owe money to a foreign government. I didn't do drugs I couldn't buy in a shop. If I had dangerous secrets, I'd kept them tight enough that there was no one left to tell. Still, the process moved so quickly. Just like that, no more Suomi.

In my new job I was one week on, two weeks off. The week I worked I was on call 24/7. Off meant off, like flipping off a switch. There were three teams working on the Elliptical polar orbit. Spy satellites. I knew nothing else, because my job was so tightly tangled in the machinery of it all that what I was actually doing was never apparent. All I had to do was let the numbers and designs become beautiful to me. The machines did what we told them to do, arrows nesting in soft things.

✳

One early evening my dog pulled me uphill, stopped to smell the trampled grass, fresh kill. That night I let him out the back door, but he wouldn't wander. Stood on the back stoop shivering, pawing the door while something yowled up in the tangle.

Cougar see prey in everything. I learned their sounds from YouTube videos. I'd never been afraid of ghosts, but I knew enough to feel afraid of a big cat's teeth and claws. I took the dog behind the house and banged a pot to ward off yowls. Rattled keys while he sniffed straggly bushes around the fence. In the morning, he pawed through underbrush, traced the hollow mouth of drainage pipe beneath the hill. He just liked the smell of death that wasn't his. From videos, I learned a winter need for listening.

When a big cat comes for you, you'll know.
Stare into her eyes. Don't turn your back; don't run or scream.
You can't be catlike, only human: plainspoken, righteous, frozen.

✳

All January I'd worn a rash like a stain, blood-colored dots around my stomach, my breasts. This was before the first Seattle cases made big news around the world. Before the pandemic had a name, when it was just symptoms showing up in doctor's offices, in urgent care, in drug stores like the one where I bought tubes of cream to stop the itching, even though it was coming from inside. Doctors didn't know what caused the pocks or why. I had headaches that pulled my thoughts out of myself and into wilder realms of pain. I felt so tired I could barely walk. I'd take the dog outside to pee, then climb up the stairs and collapse. More than once I lay down on the rug in my hallway after unlatching my dog's leash. I'd close my eyes, stare up at the ceiling, fall asleep. Wake up when the itching became unbearable. It hit me out of nowhere and two weeks later it was nearly gone, stray red marks at my waist. I got better. Then it hit again, the same thing, slightly less intense, in February. Again in March. By then the word *pandemic* was in the public discourse; by the end of March in Seattle we were supposed to stay home. Still I didn't think, and my doctor didn't think, I'd had it. Because my breathing didn't change. Because we didn't understand its mutability, its capacity to show itself in wholly different guises from person to person. My symptoms recurred, fainter each time, until they seemed to stop at the end of the blazing hot summer of wildfires.

Not until September did my body make sense again, the stain gone, my stomach sticking out from no more gym but white skinned like dead meat as I'd been born with. I didn't fit the pattern. I didn't stop breathing, didn't feel my lungs fill with broken glass, with water, with words I couldn't say. But slowly the doctors worked around the president's disinformation campaign, worked around the lies he'd spread, his injunction to inject ourselves with disinfectant, to binge on hydroxychloroquine. Slowly doctors whispered what they knew, and it seemed I'd had the sickness all along, an early case, not unexpected given how the unknown illness spread in Seattle before we knew, when we were still eating in restaurants, drinking in bars, fucking on the bed, on the sofa, on the floor in front of the sliding glass door that led to my balcony. My last lover's name was Jessie. It didn't last; we had nothing to talk about. We stopped sleeping together before the stay at home orders. By that time, I was really alone.

✳

I always thought she'd come back, my wife. Still I said *my wife*, as if she was. As if the word *ex* would change the past as well as the future. I thought we'd come back simultaneously, like orgasms but cooking dinner together. Suddenly Ada and I would be married again.

Instead I got an invitation. It was August, or at least it wasn't September. Ada sent it to my Seattle address; it was forwarded to the cabin. The envelope was pale yellow, not lemon but a sugary dry color. I knew right away. *How could she,* I thought, which was stupid. How could she not? My friends said the pandemic was rushing everyone toward something they maybe didn't really want. Here I was in the woods, worrying about being mauled by a cougar, worrying a tree would crush me in my sleep, eating canned soup from someone else's kitchen, talking earnestly to my dog about the political situation while my ex-wife was running around Seattle trying on engagement rings with her very loud and not particularly funny paramour grabbing her elbow through the plaid of her sleeve.

I sent the RSVP card back right away. It was shaped like a mask. You could check *I will attend and stand 6 feet away* or *I can't make it but I'm sending a gift.* I checked nothing, just wrote STAY SAFE in red marker at the bottom of the card.

The red marker dripped a little on the E.

I took my ski pole off its hat hook by the door. I leashed the dog and masked up. I set out. I walked until I saw a doe and two new baby deer, small as puppies, fuzzy and spotted.

✳

Then nothing happened for a few days and I ran out of soup.

✳

I drove into town. I had two masks, one the cute fabric kind and one the ugly surgery kind. I put the cute mask over the ugly mask. I had hand sanitizer, but not the lotion kind, because it didn't work as well. I had hot tea in a thermos because supposedly if you drank hot liquid after getting the virus in your mouth, the hot liquid would wash the virus down your throat and the way your throat skin or blood or whatever worked would kill the virus but not kill you. Also I liked tea.

The parking lot felt strange, like going home after moving away forever. I expected to see my parents in the grocery store, sitting together on apple crates, holding hands and selling candy apples. Instead there was a teenager sanitizing shopping carts, spraying them with abandon, polishing them like he'd polish a car, and another teenager handing out masks to people who'd forgotten or refused to wear them. Someone tried to argue with the mask up teenager. Something about conspiracy theories and the president's red hat. I'd had it already and I hadn't even made it into the store. Got in a fight with conspiracy dude. We were both thrown out. I still needed soup, so I walked a few blocks to the other grocery store, the expensive one bought out by the big corporation.

Everyone there was wearing a mask, moving in cautious circles around the store, giving each other space. Whispering, "Thank you" to employees. One white woman bowed and made prayer hands at a man who was stacking bunches of carrots next to parsnips. He ignored her. She edged over and tried to thank him in the face and he just stepped away, afraid. It was so clear that no one knew what the fuck to do with themselves. I bought a can of expensive soup and a slice of non-dairy cake because I'd spent so much time researching factory farming that now I could only eat plant-based food without weeping for the baby cows.

Then I switched my masks around and went back to the normal grocery store I'd been 86'd from. They let me in. Our memories weren't working the way they used to. They thought I was someone new, someone in a surgery mask. Or maybe they were secretly glad I'd shouted at the red hat dude. I filled my basket with soup and pasta and coffee and cereal and apples and bags of frozen vegetables. I bought pickled vegetables labeled *RAW PROBIOTIC* because I liked the word *BIOTIC*. It reminded me of The Bionic Man and The Bionic Woman. For a moment I got lost in childhood, orange shag carpeting, rec rooms, striped shirts, and Zoom the TV show. I could still do the weird little thing with my arms. I hummed the Zoom song under my breath. An attractive white man-woman couple looked at me, maskless faces crinkled up, like I smelled bad, which maybe I did.

✳

Days went by, and nothing happened. It was one of my off weeks. I didn't know what to do with myself. I wrote long texts to my ex-wife, demanding an explanation, reminding her that she'd told me herself that her now new wife wasn't nearly as good in bed as I was and that she faked it when they used the strap on. I sent the texts to myself, a trick my therapist had invited me to try, except maybe once I messed up and actually sent it. Well, maybe twice. When I told this to my therapist a few days later in our Zoom therapy session, she laughed, a thing I liked about her: that she could laugh with me. Only then something weird happened. I realized she wasn't laughing. No sound came out of her mouth. She shook.

"Are you okay?" I asked.

She petted her therapy dog, Demon. He'd tried to bite me once, in The Before Times. She was crying, but keeping it very close to laughing, and I knew if I left her alone for a minute, she'd rein it all back in.

We both pretended to be looking at ourselves onscreen. Really I was looking at her. She was so pretty, a straight lady. I'd picked her because she was so married and straight, and I knew no matter how hard I turned on my charms, no matter how much I projected out or in, it wouldn't matter. But now I just wanted her to feel better.

It was a thing that kept happening. I'd go somewhere necessary, like the gas station or the grocery store, or I'd log onto a Zoom meeting or a work call, and inevitably someone, sometimes someone strong, would crack. I came to recognize the silence, the tilt of the head. If it was a busy Zoom call, the person would just disappear, leaving their avatar sipping coffee, kayaking, or smiling blandly in front of a bookcase. Some people had photos of their pets. The more pet photos I saw in a meeting, the worse things were.

✳

The rains returned overnight in September. When I walked by the lake, Theo dug up the same sticks he'd buried days earlier. Geese honked, flying in perfect formation over the water, swooping in unison. At the far edge of the lake was a golf course, the landscape's one unchanging world. White men in pastel shirts, golf carts, silver clubs, balls that inevitably flew into the water. Occasionally deer high-stepped it across the green, holding up the game as if they knew exactly what they were doing.

One off-week afternoon I let Theo run free. He disappeared into the woods after a squirrel. I stumbled through brush, calling *Theo! Theodore Henry!* Through the forest, onto a road I hadn't realized existed. There was Theo, looking pleased with himself for running his own adventure. Behind him was a house, no neighbors, no street signs. Two stories, modern, white and gray. It fit perfectly within the trees, against the sky, against the ravine on one side and the hill on the other. I stared up at the window and that was when I saw the man.

The man saw me and waved.

I waved back.

Then I called to Theo, and we walked away from the house, up a dirt road covered with stones. I realized I'd passed it before, not realizing it was a road. It didn't seem to have a name. We walked back along the lake while the golfers golfed and a heron stood silently among the reeds.

✳

I felt my restlessness returning. I texted a few friends to ask if anyone was dating. Their answers were: *Yes. Strange. Chaste.* Phone dates, Zoom dates, dates standing far apart in parks. I downloaded an app and swiped. I chatted. I met up.

Her name was Selena and she was a professor at the university in town. We met in a park, both masked, wearing thick coats because of the chill. The wind blew her skirt lightly around her ankles. When she talked about teaching, I could see that thing some teachers have for their students: a core compassion and concern.

"But I'm not a pushover," she said. "I'm a tough grader."

"Do I get an A?"

"You? We just met."

Before the pandemic hit, she'd been midway through writing a book about the impact of social media on social justice movements.

"Now I need to add a chapter on Zoom."

"Do people actually use Zoom for activism?"

She shook her head. "It's not that Zoom is a distribution tool the way Facebook and Twitter are. It's that the way people talk to other people on Zoom—controlling privacy settings, for example, or using an avatar instead of a live feed—impacts their social media use."

"So it's happening in reverse?"

"Yeah. Social media impacts activism, but the way people are using social media is starting to change. So I'm wondering how that will impact activism and looking at Zoom lets me make predictions."

All this talking was a turn on for me. It was the first face-to-face intellectual conversation I'd had in months.

"Can I hug you?" I said.

She looked taken aback.

"I'm sorry. That was probably inappropriate." I shifted from foot to foot nervously.

She stared into the distance. The park where we were walking was close to the water, near a sewage treatment plant. People called it the Sewage Treatment Plant neighborhood. It was really nice. The houses all had little gardens. There were lots of rainbow flags and Black Lives Matter signs and bumper stickers for non-fascist political candidates.

"I'd like that," she said.

Neither one of us moved.

Finally, I gestured for her to step toward me, and she did. I wrapped my arms around her puffy coat. I could feel the small of her back through fabric. I closed my eyes. I thought she closed hers, but her face was buried against my shoulder. My face mask got damp and stuck to my mouth. It felt like the most forbidden thing I could imagine.

Suddenly a dog barked, and its person shouted, "Scooby," in a way that let us know someone had seen us and was approaching. The person looked so apologetic, or at least, their eyes did, and the wide circle they made around us, twenty feet at least.

Selena stepped back.

"Thank you," I said, because I didn't know what else to say.

She looked like she might cry. "Can I see your whole face? If we back up and stand at least twelve feet away?"

I nodded. We walked backwards, as if we were in a duel or trying not to startle an animal. "Tell me when," I said, and she did, and when I saw her mouth, I thought no one could ever be more beautiful.

That night I texted her:
I'd really like to see you again.
I watched while bubbles percolated:
I'll keep your number if you keep mine.

✳

I thought I'd text Selena. I thought she'd text me. But things kept getting worse out in the real world, spiraling, and I guess we both forgot. As the days passed I felt trapped in some forgotten myth, as if I might turn to salt if I looked back, if I let myself remember.

One night while I was boiling water for pasta my phone rang. I answered without checking to see who was calling.

"Hi. How are you doing?" It was Ada. Before I could answer, she launched into a gushy speech, thanking me for sending monogrammed organic cotton bathrobes as a wedding gift.

"I didn't, though."

She just kept talking about the wedding, the gifts, everything so perfect, so wonderful. What a shame I couldn't make it. How much I would've enjoyed the location, waterfront, the tide nearly splashing the floral arbor. The flower girls and their pastel dresses. The ringbearer dog. Sunset over the sea.

"I didn't send you bathrobes. That's not a thing I would do."

"Oh." There was a pause. She said my name—"Quinn"—and for a split second I thought I heard affection. Then the tone I'd grown used to, a different voice, not the voice of the woman I'd married in Canada, before it was legal here, and then remarried when it finally was. Now all of that was up in the air, the government turning against its people once more, history reeling its cinematic landscape backward, my wife's voice disappearing into the voice of a woman who asked, "What did you send us?"

I'd sent coffee cups. She drank coffee all day long, using a new cup every time. I started to say that, then thought better of it.

"I made a donation in your name."

Disappointment rang through her voice. "I see."

"You know we're going to have human composting soon, right? The Governor signed the bill and everything. So I made a donation to a human composting science center in Seattle."

"You're kidding."

"I thought you'd be honored to contribute to scientific research. They're studying corpses at the Body Farm. Bringing the technology here to Seattle."

"Fuck you."

"It's science, Ada. You'll always be a part of it now."

"You ruin everything, Quinn. I'm finally in love and you want to talk about corpses at some farm? Why can't you just be happy for me?"

"The Body Farm. It's a specific place. They let bodies decompose there. To study them."

"I hate you."

"You married me."

"I don't even remember you. It's like it never happened."

"You're the one who called to thank me for buying you a wedding gift. And got it wrong, Ada."

"Because I thought you bought us something nice. Cute monogrammed bathrobes."

"Science is nice. Human composting is nice. I bet you two want to be buried, don't you? Do you know how wasteful that is?"

"You're the worst, Quinn. You compartmentalize everything. Just like your job. You want to pretend all you're doing is math, but the big picture is drones and surveillance and missiles and assassinations and God knows what else. It's not science. It's murder."

"I bought you coffee cups."

She hung up.

∗

I was tired and decided it was time to turn into a tree.

Wasn't this how it happened in myths, in fairy tales? I'd go into the forest and come back changed. I'd find a wolf, a huntsman, a magic chalice, a ring. I'd stand still for so long that my limbs sprouted greenery and I swayed in sync with roots wrapped round my ankles, pulsing for water, until I was that thirsty tree.

I stood next to a pine. I stood next to a birch. I lay down under an oak. Two squirrels fought their way around a mossy log. I heard birds calling to each other or talking about me. Or maybe talking to themselves the way I'd started to do, first occasionally, now full-blown paragraphs, commenting on everything I did, chatting myself up, narrating a life no one else was close to. As if speaking the words in my head would connect me to some human story. As if it might ward off disease or the loneliness I was starting to think might be much, much worse.

✳

Without meaning to, Theo and I found ourselves back in front of the hidden house, waving again at the man inside. He looked pleasantly amused, glancing up from a laptop positioned so he could see out into the woods. As I turned to hike back home, I noticed a hornet's nest nearly hidden beneath the eaves. I hesitated, then doubled back, masked up, and knocked on his door.

"There's a hornet's nest," I said. "Up there, under your roof."

He nodded. "I called the Department of Agriculture. In case it's murder hornets."

I'd forgotten the murder hornets. There were so many ways for things to spiral out of control. "Good luck with all that."

"Thank you. And thank you, Theo." He shut the door.

Theo and I walked home along the lake.

✳

I spent much of my time thinking about surveillance. I knew that the technology I worked on could be used to do great things, like help people evacuate before a hurricane hit; or terrible things, like pinpoint people in precise locations and bomb them to smithereens. It felt like the price of admission, not just for my job, but for moving through the world as it was now: cameras and mics on our phones and in our houses, all the tech companies offering us new landscapes of knowledge and communication, while simultaneously monitoring our every move.

Jessie texted me. It was the exact moment when every single person's last lover texted them out of loneliness. I knew this because it was all over Twitter, where things seemed to happen in sync, maybe because I'd curated my feed to reflect my chaotic reality. Jessie and I hadn't talked since we broke up, since I found out she was running a live cam empire out of her studio apartment in Ballard.

"You said you worked in tech."

"I do."

"You get paid to live stream naked women."

"And you think that's separate from tech?"

"Why didn't you just tell me you were running a live cam operation? Did you think I would judge?"

"You're judging me now. Look, everything has its moment. The moment you share your childhood secrets, the moment you talk about food allergies, the moment you open up about kinks. I wasn't withholding; I was just waiting for moments that never came."

After the pandemic hit and everyone was trapped inside, not touching, I figured one of us would break and suggest a little friends with benefits situation. But it wasn't going to be me. I was friends with benefits with trees. I loved slugs now. I was different.

What's up? Jessie texted.

Not much. Still breathing.

Want to hang out?

There's a deadly disease we could give each other if we stand closer than six feet apart.

I know. I'm just lonely.

Me too.

We could risk it. I mean, we're both careful people.

Sorry, Jessie. Call me sometime?

Of course she never did. Talking on the phone had become strangely intimate, like sending long emails. She wasn't looking for intimacy. I just knew the thought of more cameras, more bodies onscreen, more images burned into my retina wasn't what I needed. I kept trying to imagine a landscape without a lens, my body touching another body that wasn't for the camera. The pandemic had broken the last few barriers we had between surveillance and domestic space. All day long I spoke into a screen, exercised from a screen, watching faces onscreen. The camera followed me everywhere. I wanted something real. But who was I, with my job a giant spinning eye, to ask for privacy?

✳

A few days later I was reading on the sofa, Theo curled up beside me. It was morning, sunny and cold outside. I was finishing my coffee when a knock startled us both. Theo ran to the door and barked. I picked up the heavy flashlight I kept by the door.

"Who's there?" I asked, pulling back the curtains slightly.

A tall white man stood on the doorstep. It was the man from the hidden house, the man who waved. I felt confused. How did he know where I lived? Did I know him from somewhere else?

"Sorry, I'm busy," I said through the door. "You'll have to come back later."

"I can't," he said.

"Please leave. I'm not letting you in."

"Your boss sent me."

That did not sound good. "Prove it."

He began reciting things about me only my employer knew. As I listened to the list, I felt myself shrinking. A list of facts, dates, projects I'd worked on. Code names, acronyms, salary, perks.

"Put on your mask," and we both did. Then I opened the door and stepped outside.

"I was just sent to give you this," handing me a sheet of paper. "It's your security clearance. You'll get a badge in the mail in a few weeks, but they wanted you to know you'd passed. Soon you can start working on the real project."

"Which is?"

"No idea." He shrugged, and I knew he was telling the truth. "This is all I do. This part. I'm just the man in the window. I wave. My wave sets everything in motion. It's an important job and I'm well compensated. Sometimes I get lonely but they send me books to read each week. You're lucky they let you have a dog. I asked for a cat, but they sent me a cactus. It is sad, though. About your wife."

"My ex-wife. I'm divorced."

"You don't know?"

I stared at him and shook my head.

He moved slightly to the right. Made an almost imperceptible gesture and I stepped away from the door. We walked into the yard and stood beside a tree.

"They created the divorce."

"What are you talking about?"

"Nothing that's happened to you or me was left to chance." He turned, motioned toward the house. "See the hornet's nest?"

I had one, too.

"The camera is in the nest. There are cameras inside the cabin, too. Try to understand. You're not making choices. You think you are, but you're not. They're in charge of everything. And once you're in, you're in. You can't leave. The best you can hope for is to ask for things. Like a house. I wanted a dog, a cat. I wanted a lover. But they gave me a house and it's something. They send me books every week. Not the books I ask for, but books just the same."

I thought of my Canadian friend. "The friend who's letting me stay in his cabin. Is he in on it?"

The man laughed, but not because anything was funny. His laughter reminded me of my therapist, shaking on our Zoom call, petting her dog.

"I take it the answer is yes."

"There's nothing outside of this." His voice caught in his throat. "The one thing they didn't count on was the pandemic. It's the wrench in their plans. So they've gotten a little sloppy about the details. Like your friend loaning you his cabin. Like you meeting me by chance in the woods."

"What do we do?"

"We?"

"Now that we know. Now that both of us are in on the secret."

His face changed. "There's no *we* here. There's just you in your house and me in mine. We never had this conversation." He stepped back in front of the hornet's nest.

"Is it fake? I mean, are there real hornets?"

"What do you think?" He got into his car and drove away.

I went inside and checked every lock on every door and window. Then I looked down at the piece of paper he'd given me, my security clearance. It was blank.

✳

After he left, I made lunch, cutting carrots to put in the soup. I realized I'd stopped my patterns, stopped the few things I'd tried to hold onto. Had I texted my friends every three days? Were they still receiving my texts? Were my friends still alive?

I put the pan of soup in the sink and turned off the burner. Drank two glasses of water. Polished my glasses with spit on my sleeve. Then I threw a few things in a bag, as if I might be going hiking. I put Theo in the car and we drove the winding roads towards town. I filled up the tank. I masked up and bought a backpack full of groceries. Leaning against the car I ate an apple and a handful of pumpkin seeds.

When I started the ignition, for a split second I imagined the car blowing up, like on TV when the hero is just about to make her escape. Instead the last song I'd listened to blared from the speakers. I turned the car onto the highway and drove toward Canada.

∗

When I got close to the border, I called my friend. The phone rang and rang. Finally he answered.

"Thanks so much for letting me use the cabin," I said. "I love it here. I think I'm going to stay awhile. Probably months. Maybe another year."

"That's a great idea," he said.

"How are things over the border? How's the polycule?"

He talked for a little while. I listened for clues, clicks, shifts in his tone, a rasp in his breathing, anything. Our conversation was ordinary. We hung up.

I turned onto a rural road when I got to Blaine. Pulled off on the shoulder, tried to think what I should do next. Then the phone rang, a number I didn't recognize.

I answered. It was my friend the Canadian. His voice was quiet. "The border crossing you want is the truck crossing. It's in Lynden." He hung up.

My car was pointed toward Lynden. I had enough gas to make it to the crossing. If I was right about my friend, my story would begin there. Something would happen. They couldn't see everything, they couldn't hear everything, they couldn't control every single breath I took. But if I was wrong? If I got caught trying to flee the country, with all the knowledge I had?

I let the dog out for a moment. Let him sniff, pee, get excited about a squirrel. I stood in trees at the edge of a field. Then I opened the trunk, slung my bags over my shoulders, and started walking away from the car. Theo and I walked fast, sticking to the tree line, until the car disappeared, and we were thick with shadow. Then I turned on the burner phone I'd kept for just this moment and dialed the woman I knew would answer.

Selena sounded sleepy.

"Did I wake you up?"

"No, I was grading papers and sort of losing steam. It's nice to hear from you. We dropped the ball, didn't we Quinn?"

I had to trust somebody. If I was wrong, I'd get myself out of whatever corner I'd gotten myself into. But going it completely alone wasn't an option.

"Any interest in a second date?"

"Sure. I'd like that."

"It'll be an adventure."

"I'm up for it."

Later, when she asked me how I knew I could trust her, I explained it was her sadness. The thing no one else seemed willing to show. She asked how I knew where to cross the border, how I got us under the radar and over to the other side. I explained about the satellites, how I'd helped make them. How they did good things and terrible things, too. How all along I'd been tracking, not just the weather.

We stood in a field on the other side. Theo tugged a little on the leash. Selena and I could see the lights of the boardwalk by the bay in White Rock. It was dark and we started walking. She didn't have to tell me not to stop. I didn't have to tell her not to turn around, not to look back.

SELENA SWIPES RIGHT

We stood under an awning on a deserted street, torrential rain drumming above and around us. At my feet, a wooden crate. We called it a coffee shop. We called it a date.

In the parking lot, I asked you to take it off. We backed away from each other, the requisite stance. A little more distance to survive the illness our breath might make. We stripped the masks from our faces. Mouths appeared, a magic trick.

Yes to a walk in the rain on the beach near the marina. You explained fly fishing.

I winced: how fish feel pain. There are so many ways to tear a lip. To rip a living thing, then let it slide into the deep. You loved the sailboats, seven in sync, learning how to right the craft. Your dog shivered in the chill. We stood together wanting more. We couldn't kiss but let our puffy coat sleeves rub for sparks, touching elbows in the parking lot. We never let our faces near or looked into each other's eyes. Our masks grew damp with words we didn't say.

A car pulled up beside us in the lot. A family tumbled out and stared. White man, white woman, child, infant. The children quiet, learning.

This is queer history, too. We've always touched in public because we had nowhere to go. We've always fucked the ways we could with what we couldn't lose.

That night we held our phones alone in separate rooms.

We still have dinner in a restaurant.

We still have a first kiss, waiting like a ghost.

SUNSET PRETENDS ITS HEART IS ON FIRE

Ben found out his wife was leaving from a sticky note she placed by the sink:

Out of coffee!
I want a divorce ☹
Back @ 6

The first thing Ben thought about was the "at" sign. Wasn't that an abbreviation reserved for texting? It was a complicated character to draw. Ben doubted Aster had saved herself any time at all by scrawling a circle around a lower case "a" instead of writing "a" and "t." The second thing Ben thought about was the exclamation mark. Was it supposed to be funny that they'd run out of coffee? Or did the exclamation mark mean Aster was frustrated or angry? The third thing Ben thought about was the frown emoji following the word "divorce," a word he didn't think about at all because he couldn't.

When Aster returned from the store, he followed her around the kitchen while she put away groceries. Then he followed her into their bedroom, where she stuffed clothes into an overnight bag.

"Whatcha doing?" Ben leaned against the doorframe and looked down at his feet.

"Did you get my note?"

"Did you get coffee?" Ben meant it as a joke, but Aster didn't laugh. "I didn't mean that in a sexist way."

"I know."

"Do you want to binge watch one of your food shows? I'll make dinner. We can just hang out."

"Do you want to talk about my note?"

"There's nothing to talk about." As soon as Ben said the words, he wanted to rearrange or delete them. He meant that he didn't want to talk about coffee or ampersands or exclamation marks. He also didn't want to talk about the word "divorce," which he couldn't say or think about, and which he was pretending he'd misread.

"Okay." Aster picked up her bag and walked past him, into the hall.

"Where are you going?"

"I thought you said there wasn't anything to talk about."

"Aster, please."

"Fine." She dropped her bag, walked into the living room, and flopped down on the sofa. "Let's talk, then."

"I'm sorry. I just don't—"

"Ben, I don't love you anymore."

"You don't have to love me."

"I know. And I don't."

"But we're married. We're roommates, too. We eat dinner together. We adopted a dog."

"I want a divorce."

This time the words hit Ben with full force. He opened his mouth, but no sound came out. He stood rooted to the floor while Aster looked at her fingernails. Right now they were pink, with white at the tips. Ben thought about her hands, how much he loved to hold them, how much he loved looking at the wedding ring on her finger. How his wedding ring felt like part of his body. He never took it off, not even at the gym.

Aster stood up. "Someday you'll understand." She picked up her bag and walked out the door.

✳

Ben stood in the living room, looking at the door, breathing the air she'd left behind. At some point, minutes or maybe hours later, their dog began to whine. Ben looked at Scooby and consoled him by singing a song he'd made up to celebrate Scooby's adoption years earlier. Scooby looked uncomfortable, as he often did when Ben was too devoted. Nonetheless he allowed Ben to sink his face into his fur, to cry loudly, to talk to him as if they shared the same limited human vocabulary of pain.

"I don't know if she's coming back for you, buddy," Ben said, as much to himself as to Scooby. Then he noticed that Aster had taken exactly half of the face masks they kept hanging on hooks by the front door. Ben started crying again.

Aster didn't come home that night or the next night. Ben had been trying to play it cool, give her space, but then he began to worry she might want him to coax her back. She'd never left before, never said the word "divorce," so it didn't feel like a trick. But what if it was a test? Ben broke down and texted:

Come home!

We miss you.

That's me and Scooby btw.

He felt better then. He'd expressed his feelings, the way she was always asking him to do, the way he tried to do, although he never seemed to get it right.

His phone pinged and he checked his texts:

Scooby loves you more. ☹

You can keep him. ☺

My lawyer will be in touch. ☹

Ben continued to be confused by Aster's new use of emoji. Had something shifted inside her, a change in the symbolic order of her world?

✳

Ben spent a month forgetting things that reminded him of Aster. He forgot to drink coffee in the morning and developed splitting headaches. He forgot to turn on the TV and sat watching the blank screen. He forgot to take T, panicking a few days later when he noticed the unused syringe. He forgot to wear a mask to the grocery store, where he was turned away at the automatic doors. Ben stood outside in the parking lot, trying to understand why he'd been stared at and shamed out of the store. Then he remembered the pandemic. He felt briefly happy that he'd forgotten something so terrible, yet integral to daily life. It was as if in order to forget the word "divorce," Ben had to forget the life he'd built around their marriage. He wondered if he could just forget Aster. If he could remember to drink coffee, wear a mask, move through the world as he always had, but without Aster. The space beside him quiet, serene.

The phone rang exactly a month after Aster walked out. Ben didn't recognize the number but picked up just in case.

"Hello?"

"It's Aster."

"I miss you. Scooby and I have been stress eating. Come home and we can do whatever you want."

"I'm not coming home, Ben. Do you have a lawyer yet?"

Ben resisted the urge to say, "What for?" He knew what for, and also didn't know, and also wished he hadn't answered the phone.

"Ben? Are you there?"

"I don't have a lawyer."

"You need to get one. My lawyer needs to talk to your lawyer. I'm trying to make this as easy as possible. You need to hold up your end. I can't do this by myself."

"I don't want a divorce." How could she ask him to hold up his end of something he didn't want in the first place?

"I know you don't." It was the first time Aster's voice had sounded compassionate, or something like it. "But I do. It takes two people to make a marriage."

Ben's shoulders tightened. What he'd liked about Aster, why he'd married her, was that she was different. They both laughed at everything, especially sad or horrifying things. They were both weird. Now she was spouting clichés about marriage and calling from a phone number he didn't recognize.

"Do you want to go to a counselor? Maybe we could talk this out. I don't even know what's wrong."

"Ben." Her voice was faintly warm, like a stovetop just turned off. "Please call a lawyer. Let's just get through this. It'll be easier on the other side, I promise."

Ben could hear her breathing. Aster was a heavy breather. He'd always liked it, liked how even when she was quiet, he knew she was close. But now it just sounded ugly, as if she was in a hostage situation.

"Are you seeing someone else?"

Nothing. Ben listened to the refrigerator's little burps, which sounded almost human.

"I'm not going to be mad, Aster. I just want to know."

"Yes." All of her bossiness disappeared into the "s" at the end of the word.

"Do you want to tell me when it started?"

"Not really."

"Do you want to tell me who it is?"

"Ben."

"I'm listening."

"It's not someone who—I mean—I mean it doesn't matter. That's not why I want a divorce."

"Can you at least tell me their name, so I don't make small talk with them in the grocery store?"

Aster breathed more heavily than usual. Then she said Ben's best friend's name. Ben thought about his friend, and what it meant to have a friend he could confide in. How he'd called his best friend 4 or 5 times since Aster left. While Ben was thinking about his friend, he felt comfort. His thoughts about his friend occurred separately from the rising anger he felt toward Aster. In his brain, he was thinking happy thoughts about his best friend while Aster named his best friend as the answer to a question, but the two things didn't correlate.

"Are you okay?" she asked.

Ben hung up.

He googled "divorce lawyer," carefully setting the map to a 20 mile radius. It seemed like the correct amount of space, and besides, that way he knew he wouldn't get suggestions across the border, in Canada, which would do him no good. He couldn't even cross the border; the U.S. was quarantined from the rest of the world because the President had mismanaged virus containment in outlandish, terrifying ways. This was the sort of thing Ben and his best friend talked about a lot, in text, on the phone, over a few beers.

Ben looked at his phone and tapped his best friend's contact information. He didn't have the phone number or email address memorized, because his phone did all that for him. He looked at the number for a second, then forced himself to look away. Then he blocked and deleted the contact.

✳

Scooby seemed lethargic. He wasn't eating as much as usual and wouldn't fetch his plush elephant. Ben took Scooby to the vet, where they waited in the car because no one was allowed inside. Eventually a vet tech came to the car to take Scooby away. It was the worst feeling. Ben couldn't explain to Scooby that there was a pandemic raging, and anyone might be an asymptomatic carrier. Instead he let a stranger in a mask and gloves take Scooby's leash and lead him away.

"I'm getting a divorce," Ben said to the vet tech as she clipped the leash on Scooby's collar. "My wife left me for my best friend. I deleted their contact information, though."

The vet tech looked at Ben, an unreadable expression since her mouth was covered. Ben smiled back under his mask, but the fabric inner layer sucked into his mouth, leaving fuzz on his tongue.

Ben turned the ignition off and put his head down the steering wheel. He felt like giving up. He closed his eyes and drifted into angry daydreams. About twenty minutes later his phone pinged. The vet was texting him. They texted back and forth about Scooby. It was hard not to talk about personal things. Texting always felt intimate, even with bots or doctors. Ben restrained himself. In the end, the vet found nothing.

Your dog feels your stress. ☹
You're worried, your dog is worried. ☹
You're unhappy, your dog is unhappy. ☹
My advice to you is to be happy again. ☺
If that's not possible, take your dog for more walks. ☺

When Ben and Scooby got home, he made two peanut butter sandwiches: one for Scooby and one for himself. They ate side-by-side on the couch. It felt nice, like having a roommate. All of a sudden he realized Scooby was his roommate. Seeing Scooby this way changed things for Ben. He wasn't alone, and in fact, his roommate cared so much about his emotional state that he'd become sick just because Ben wasn't happy.

"Thank you," Ben said to Scooby. They watched a movie together.

The next morning Ben decided to walk Scooby four times, the way the vet suggested, instead of just letting him out in the yard. On the first walk, Scooby went bananas, jerking Ben around on the leash, walking him. But by walk number three Scooby was more interested in sniffing. He seemed happier, calmer that night. Ben felt calmer, too.

A few days later Ben realized there was a dog park in his neighborhood. He'd gone to the lake to eat his lunch outside; while he was sitting at a picnic table, he noticed several large dogs loping around the far end of the park. He walked over to the small wooden sign in the grass: *Off-Leash Dog Area*. Ben watched while dogs ran in great magic loops. This, he thought, was what Scooby needed. It was also what Ben needed. He could stand at the shore of the lake and listen to geese while Scooby ran with a pack.

That night he told Scooby he would take him to the park very soon. He wanted Scooby to have something to dream about. They both ate vanilla ice cream side-by-side on the couch and watched TV. Ben remembered a few things he'd forgotten: to pay the electric bill, to take out the recycling. He felt his memory lighting up again. He felt words form easily speaking to Scooby.

"Soon," he said, "we'll go to the dog park. It's a park especially for dogs like you."

Scooby tilted his head as if he understood. He was a great roommate. Ben let him have the last bit of ice cream.

While he washed dishes, Ben looked up at the calendar hanging over the sink. He and Aster both liked keeping a paper calendar. Writing things down made them feel more real and helped him remember. He noticed something then, a pattern. Aster had written *Book Club* once a week, on Wednesday nights, for the past two months. But she didn't belong to a book club. He knew this because she talked to her mother every day and her mother often encouraged her to read more. Aster would always sigh and say she didn't have time.

Ben wondered if *Book Club* meant something else. If she'd thought he was stupid, missing clues left and right. He remembered asking her if she'd changed her shampoo, wondering why she'd started drinking. He dunked the ice cream bowls in sudsy water, dried them off with one of the dish towels he'd picked out when they moved into the apartment almost three years ago. The lease would be up in two months. Ben texted Aster to ask what she planned to do.

Call please ☺

Ben understood that it was the sort of thing that would take too long in text, at least according to the Aster-sphere, whose rules of conduct had been ingrained in Ben until he forgot that they were never his rules. But he also knew that he didn't want to hear Aster's voice, that hearing her voice might undo the progress he and Scooby were making to deal with reality.

Ben decided to try something new. He texted:

I'd rather not ☺

The little bubbles started immediately and went on for a very long time. Finally, Aster texted back:

I'm engaged and I live here now.

You can keep the furniture. ☺

Ben tried to think but his brain was also making little bubbles, as if he was waiting to speak words that might come from somewhere else.

You can't be engaged. ☹

You're still married to me. ☺

Aster didn't reply. Ben waited and waited, even just for bubbles, but the screen went blank.

＊

The next time Ben saw Aster, they both had face masks on, and so did their lawyers. They sat at a table, four adults wearing masks printed in cheerful patterns, as if they were at a costume party and not starting divorce paperwork. Nothing about the hour in the lawyer's office reminded him of divorce scenes in movies. It was emotionally devastating, but slow, with no dignity or interesting speeches. Midway through the meeting, Ben realized that he might never see Aster again without a face mask on. She wasn't in his pandemic pod anymore and neither was his best friend. His pandemic pod consisted of two people, and they had just run off with each other.

Ben stabbed his pen onto the notepad the lawyer had placed in front of him, as if he was a child who required a coloring book. Then he stopped, because Aster's lawyer was staring. Aster leaned over and whispered something into her lawyer's ear.

"Why are you talking about me?" Ben's voice sounded murky beneath his mask. "You slept with my best friend."

"Fiancé," Aster corrected him. "My fiancé."

Ben felt his soul leave his body, or maybe it was the inner lining of his mask sticking to his tongue again. He looked down at the notepad. He'd drawn a heart with *Scooby* inside. If Ben had to choose between Scooby and his best friend, he'd choose Scooby every time.

Ben looked at Aster, or the part of Aster's face he could see above her mask: eyes, forehead, hair pulled back with a clip. He tried to feel love, then grief, then rage, but the only thing he felt was nothing. Aster was someone else now, as if the Aster he'd loved had been replaced with a bot.

*

For a few days, Ben believed maybe Aster had been replaced with a bot. It made it easier to think this way. He imagined the moment the switch had happened. Maybe he'd brought her coffee in bed, a second cup, because she always liked to drink from a new cup, and she drank a lot of coffee. Ben thought maybe it happened while he was standing in the kitchen, pouring from the leaky coffee pot, wiping spilled coffee with his pajama sleeve. She was taken. Just snatched up. So this meant real Aster was still out there somewhere, floating around the universe with an empty cup, wondering why he was taking so long.

Ben put a tennis ball in his coat pocket. Called Scooby and snapped on the leash.

"Let's go to the dog park. You can run and jump and be a dog."

Scooby said nothing. Ben didn't mind. He just kept talking. He told Scooby everything now. Told him Aster's fingernails looked ridiculous. Told him anything could happen. The door was wide open. What door? Ben imagined Scooby saying, confused. Why Scooby, the door to the future of love.

When they arrived at the dog park, it was empty. The sky was shifting from eggshell to violet to an ominous shade of blue that Ben did not like. It began to hail. At first the hail looked like snow, then salt, then shards of glass, then misshapen golf balls. Ben pulled his jacket over his head. Then he saw Scooby.

Scooby was a puppy again. He ran into the hail, then let it chase him. Snapped his jaw and ate big bites. Pushed through the misshapen golf balls, then ran after them full tilt. The hail kept flinging itself at Scooby and Scooby flung himself back just as hard. Everything glittered, a shivering wave. Ben stood on the sand with his shoes touching the water. The ominous blue melted into something softer, velvet where it met the lake.

PEEPHOLE

1. MIRA

Mira had a thing about shiny people. There were negative shiny people, too, but they weren't magical. They just had extra bad energy. Mira avoided them, but when she was forced to interact they drained her. Shiny people gave her a boost of energy, a magnetic pull.

Ben lit up the room the minute she saw him at Sadie's party. He walked in the door and he was just shiny. Her feelings for Ben surprised her, because she'd dated women for so long that she'd forgotten she occasionally had feelings for men. A man needed to be shiny and then do everything right. Her bar was so high. For women her bar was somewhere on the floor.

"Nonexistent." Sadie had been her friend forever and could say these things. "Your bar for women is nonexistent."

It was true. Mira had dated some doozies. "Yes, but they've all been hot and good in bed."

"I'll give you that," Sadie said. They were sitting on Sadie's porch in The Before Times. Sadie was painting her fingernails.

"This is very gendered," Mira looked at her hands. "You being femme and me just watching."

"I like it when you watch." Sadie flirted with everyone, but it still felt special. Mira put her head on Sadie's shoulder. Then Sadie's partner Kate and Kate's girlfriend Lina came out on the porch and sat on the swing.

"Where's the rest of the polycule?" Mira asked.

"Richard said he'd be home by 5."

Richard was fine, but he wasn't shiny. He drank too much and mansplained Queer Theory. Mira could only handle small doses of Richard. She hugged everyone and walked home through the alley.

Back then, everyone hugged, just like saying hello.

Back then, Ben was happily married to Aster. Mira was his best friend and he told her everything. She told him everything except her feelings for him. But that was before masks and quarantine, before something shifted between Ben and Aster, before their marriage shattered into shards that cut everyone around them, too. Now everyone in their friend group knew Aster was thinking of leaving. Mira felt protective of Ben and his goofy, good-natured obliviousness. Aster had broken his heart and he didn't even know.

✳

Every morning Mira logged onto Zoom at 8:57. She needed the extra three minutes to compose her face, smooth out sleep or stress. A buttery yellow smear filled her screen, the corner of the yellow sticky note she put over the laptop camera lens. At 8:59 she took the sticky note off. Clicked the video and the audio on. Then she was in another world, a world of faces in boxes. A few coworkers she'd met, but most she didn't know. Management started the meeting promptly at 9 every day. Mira was grateful to work for prompt people. She listened, occasionally texting a friend or glancing at Facebook. She'd learned how to text without moving her shoulders. Face still, eyes straight ahead, she stared calmly into the camera while her fingers formed words.

It was Monday in the Year of the Great Pandemic. No, it was Tuesday. Mira hadn't showered since Wednesday, but which day was Wednesday? Was Wednesday today? No, today was Friday. Fridays were the worst for Mira. They implied that the weekend was coming, something to be happy about, but there was no weekend anymore. There was only time, unrolling in an endless loop, and Zoom, recording it all for replay. Sometimes now when she logged onto Zoom she automatically reached for her mask.

Mira worked for a coffee company. Not the biggest one, not the one everyone in Seattle worked for, but one of the smaller ones that hadn't been eaten up by the big one yet. The big coffee company's coffee tasted burnt, but they had great benefits for their employees. Sometimes she read the job ads wistfully. But it wasn't that easy, making the switch. Her job had nothing to do with coffee. Her job was copywriting, specifically social media marketing, and the big company had that all wrapped up. Besides, she told herself, it was more fun working for the little guy. When she came up with really clever copy or promotions, sometimes they'd actually see a bump in sales. She felt proud of this, helping people make choices. Also, the coffee was actually good.

Mira half-listened as a team member in Sacramento talked about research into car emissions at drive-through locations. A few more faces appeared onscreen from Health and Safety. Then a few baristas, talking about company representation at the annual International Barista Art Competition, another event held on Zoom this year. At 9:30 the CEO's face appeared onscreen. His Zoom box was the same size as everyone else's, but he was wearing a suit jacket and a tie. Mira still had on pajama bottoms. Everyone sat up straighter as the CEO went on and on, talking to hear himself talk. Mira drifted off, face set in a plastic smile while her mind wandered, until she heard the word "merger." They were selling the company to the bigger company. So it was true, the cloud hanging over. Now things would change, but no one knew how.

Management came back. Faces flickered on and off. Everyone would be receiving instructions to discuss next steps in the restructuring. Mira knew this meant layoffs as well as a few people climbing the ladder. She logged off Zoom, put the sticky note over the camera, splashed water on her face, changed into her softest pajamas. Called Ben and talked until it seemed like time to put a frozen pizza in the oven and watch reality TV. She was halfway through season seven of one of the dating shows. All the men looked alike and all the women were mean.

The next morning she woke up to a text from Aster. She didn't have her glasses on, so at first she thought she'd received a disaster notification. This seemed likely. Everything was a disaster lately. But it was Aster, asking if she was going to be on the call today. Mira remembered then that Aster worked for the big coffee company, in the Seattle HQ building with the mermaid logo that towered over the broken viaduct.

So glad U are joining the Team! Aster texted.

Mira wasn't sure what to say. Was she joining the Team? What was the Team? The big coffee company in general? Aster's group in particular? Had she been promoted without knowing it? What if she was being fired and Aster was just being sarcastic? Mira quickly texted back a smiley face, meaning *I don't know anything right now.* Then she did twenty minutes of yoga from the same YouTube video she watched every morning, took a shower, ate a granola bar and a handful of blueberries in front of her computer. It was 8:55, four minutes early. She breathed deeply, in and out, until it was exactly 8:59. Then she lifted the yellow sticky note from the laptop camera and waited while faces zoomed onto her screen.

The day's meeting picked up where yesterday's meeting left off. More details about the merger. Management had things to say. One by one faces from the big company joined Mira's coworkers onscreen. She understood then that something big was about to happen. They were going to be assigned to teams, new groups that fit within the larger company. This was what Aster had been talking about, she realized. She felt detached, numb. Her whole life was just a puzzle piece someone was moving around on the screen.

While Management rattled on about how the small company was adding value to the big company and the big company was bringing the small company into "the contemporary moment in coffee," Mira couldn't help but notice how bored everyone looked. Whichever company they belonged to, their faces were numb. She swiped from screen to screen, looking for Aster. There were 107 people on the call, everyone muted except Management. The CEO hadn't bothered to come back. He'd done his thing. She knew she'd probably never see him again.

Suddenly Mira heard a soft rustling sound, like a cat playing with paper. Someone's mic was on, distracting everyone just slightly. But it was just that papery sound, no matter. She checked her own mic and nervously glanced at her sweatpants; double checked to see if her button-down shirt was still buttoned. The middle button always wanted to pop because boobs. It was one of those things that she cared less about in person than on Zoom. How the middle button always eventually gave way, and the wilted ribbon in the crease of her bra showed through her shirt until she noticed it, rebuttoning the button or fixing it with a safety pin or even a stapler. In person she didn't mind, didn't even feel embarrassed. These things happened all the time.

Everyone was used to bodies back then. But now there was a way that what appeared on camera needed to be perfect. It was like bodies were divided in half, a magician's assistant sawed at the waist. Below the belt, everyone was in their underwear or sweats, barefoot or wearing the ugliest shoes, sitting on milk crates with Legos or kitty litter or crumpled candy wrappers on the floor below the screen. But above the waist everything was on camera, and everyone was secretly thinking like Room Rater, eyeing plants, bookshelves, paintings. Scrutinizing hair and make-up, shirts and jackets, ties and jewelry. Mira felt more pressure than ever to look professional, whatever that meant.

The soft papery sound grew louder. Now it sounded like footsteps but muffled or padded. Slippers maybe. Someone walking on carpet uphill. Was it kittens? Did someone have a lap full of tiny mewling creatures? Was it a fan with something caught in the blade?

Then Mira noticed someone named Brendan staring at someone's Zoom box. Of course she couldn't tell where his eyes were focused, because everyone on Zoom appeared to be looking straight at her when they were looking at themselves. Some people didn't even have the call on gallery, just on speaker, so they only saw one face at a time. But Brendan was staring at something or someone. He looked horrified, like he was watching a murder. Mira lost track of whatever management was saying. Now it wasn't just Brendan. Now it was someone named Audrey. Now it was someone with a Four Seasons Total Landscaping Zoom background. Now it was Mira's friend Tamika. Carefully, without moving her face and without shifting her forced smile, she texted Tamika.

What are U seeing?

Mira waited a few seconds, then glanced down at her phone.

Def not good. Don't scroll thru gallery.

Mira promptly scrolled through gallery. There were so many faces, names, an endless roll of bored expressions and fake smiles. But now she was seeing more and more horrified looks.

Her phone pinged. Tamika had sent her a text.

RU friends with Aster IRL?

Yes. Why?

U need to tell her the camera's still on.

Mira felt sick. She stopped scrolling, not wanting to look, but it was too late. There was Aster, a box on her screen, pants pulled down on the toilet. She was naked, a towel at her feet, and the shower beside her running. She was making faces and the soft sound was toilet paper and her pants, rustling.

Aster stood up. Mira tried to look away, but couldn't, then slammed her laptop down. Grabbed her phone. She knew in calling Aster that she would be the person to humiliate her, and that the moment Aster got the call would be recorded on this Zoom that was no doubt already going viral. Already being watched by a million eyes.

"Aster," she said, as her friend's voice answered, "Aster, your laptop camera's still on."

Mira heard Aster drop the phone. She waited a moment, then hung up.

After, I shut my laptop. Slipped it in its case and put it on the top shelf inside the closet. Took off my glasses and set them on my desk. Then I went into the bedroom, closed the door, drew the blinds, and turned off the light.

Inside the dark room I closed my eyes, but my eyes kept opening. I could still see the screen. It was as if the image had burned through my glasses, onto my retina, and would always be there, part of my vision. Was it Monday? Wednesday? I tried to hold on, but things slipped past me.

After a while I snapped on the light and took out a notebook from my nightstand. Drew a line down the middle. Both sides of the page were blank. I knew there were pills for this sort of thing, but I didn't have them. I didn't take pills and I didn't drink. No reason really, I told my friends, but that wasn't true. I had my reasons. It had always been easier to say no from the start than to try something and like it too much.

My dog woke me from a nightmare that was really happening. Clawed at the covers while I rubbed his head. I got up, walked into the kitchen. I couldn't look at my phone in its charger. What I needed was a landline, some way to reach someone who could tell me what to do. But no one had landlines now. Picking up the phone meant seeing. I was grateful Mira had called me. This wasn't new, being alone, but to be completely humiliated was something I didn't know how to handle.

The first time I felt the punch I doubled over, there in the kitchen. It happened again a few moments later, so hard and fast I thought someone was there, someone I couldn't see hitting me in the stomach again and again. I lay down on the floor. It kept happening until I curled into myself, my dog licking my hands, my face. I knew it was emotions, not my body, but the emotions were in my body, my emotions punching me.

I lay curled in a ball for however long. When it seemed to have stopped I stood up. I had no idea what time it was, but I opened the dryer and took out pajamas and a t-shirt. Went into the bathroom, turned the water on hot. Suddenly I saw a spider. Raced to turn off the water, then carried the spider out of the shower on a piece of toilet paper. I set it to rest on a plant in the kitchen. I'd heard somewhere that putting indoor spiders outside in winter wasn't kind. They were inside for a reason, the same reason we were. They needed warmth, the company of others, a quiet place to go unseen.

Now hot water. I scrubbed. The soap smelled of peppermint. It was my favorite scent and in December peppermint was everywhere, even in things it had no business minting. Hot water made me feel better, but the minute I stepped out of the shower I started remembering again. I toweled off, put lotion on my face so I would have something specific to do. Back when we could go to the gym, a million years ago, there was a woman who slathered her whole body in lotion after she showered. I tried not to watch her. I looked at the tile floor, the concrete walls, the wooden benches. I covered myself up, bra and boy shorts, jeans and a t-shirt. Black belt. Thick black leather boots.

I felt the punch before I thought the thing I was trying so hard not to think. Then all I could do was try to keep breathing through the hitting, doubled over, then on the floor, crying and curled in on myself, my dog circling me, shaking. I reached out for him, tried to console him. My face was covered in wet. It was time to shower again. I had a pattern already. This was what my days would look like.

It occurred to me to call in sick now, so I wouldn't need to call in sick tomorrow. I reached for my phone as if it was a normal thing to do and then remembered. I knew if I touched my phone, held it to my face and uncorked its shiny screen, I would see the number of notifications. No matter how fast I pressed the phone icon, I would see too much.

I thought about knocking at the apartment next door and asking if I could use their phone, but the sickness made every neighborly gesture suspect. Besides, what if I saw myself on the screen of their giant television, as I saw the president's red cap through the window when I walked the dog every night?

I picked up my phone. I turned it on. After a few seconds a photo of my dog appeared with the time and date plastered over his snout. He looked happy, laughing the way dogs do, and shaking off water.

The person I lived with, was married to, and didn't love anymore was away. Search-and-rescue up on Mount Baker. A skier buried in snow under an avalanche. I loved the hopeful mindset of search-and-rescue. There was always a chance, rough faith in good luck. A few years earlier a skier and his corgi went under. The corgi showed up four days later on the doorstep of the hotel where the skier's family was staying, waiting. The skier stayed dead, but the dog somehow unburied itself and walked the miles back to town. Sometimes sentient creatures find air pockets, know when to stay still, when to stay buried. When to shake the last ice off.

Even though I was no longer in love, even though I was trying to end it, they were who I wanted to see. To talk to. To hold. I felt so guilty about wanting more, more than the good person I'd married who hadn't changed, who was still so good.

But I did want more.

Only now I didn't want anything except to dial back time and stop the thing that had happened from happening.

Someone knocked on the door and my dog went wild.

I froze. No one ever knocked; we lived in an apartment with interior halls and a locked entry. Then I wondered if the neighbors knew, if they were stopping by to help.

I pressed my eye to the peephole. It was Mira, Mira who had a key and sometimes walked our dog while we were away. Mira, my partner's best friend. Mira, who'd been on the Zoom when it happened and knew everything. Mira, who'd called to tell me. Who'd been the only one to reach out.

Mira's mask was pulled below her chin. She bit her lip, shifted from foot to foot. She had a bowl covered with tinfoil and a paper bag. She knocked again, then stepped back. Set the bowl down next to the paper bag and disappeared from my fishbowl view. I waited until I heard the outer door shut, then stepped out into the hall.

The bowl held cookies, still warm. The bag held coffee, bread, cans of soup, a burner phone, and a greeting card.

I ripped open the card, which got sparkles all over the floor from the gray-and-pink sad-eyed kitten curled up in a basket. *So Sorry for Your Loss* in loopy script.

Dear Aster,

I'm so sorry for the loss of your dignity, but no one really has any, anyway. Call me if you want to talk. It could happen to anyone and it probably will. In a few days no one will even remember.

Love,

Mira

I stared at the word *love*. It was a strong word, a word I rarely used with people. Maybe I didn't use the word enough, because the effect of the word was electric. It wasn't that I felt better, it was that I felt alive. That was when I realized that since it happened, I'd gone numb; I felt dead inside and I wanted to die. Did I still? Yes, but at least I knew I wasn't, yet.

I ate a cookie. Chocolate chip. I could taste the sugar dissolving on my tongue and I remembered I hadn't eaten or had even a glass of water since it happened. And what time was it? And what day had it ever been?

The dog needed to be walked, so I walked him. For once wearing a mask felt comforting. I had on a hat, sunglasses, a puffy coat. Wasn't recognized. Had I thought I would be? I'd envisioned people outside, cameras and cellphones. I took a breath, exhaled wetly into my mask. When the dog and I finished our walk, I took off my mask and stood in the kitchen drinking cold coffee.

I turned off my phone, where the world lived.

Just then the phone rang. Which made no sense. Then I remembered the burner phone in the grocery bag. I picked up.

"Aster, it's Mira. I'm worried about you."

I couldn't talk.

"Look, you don't have to say anything, okay? Can I just come over and sit with you? I know Ben's gone. He told me about the avalanche. He'll probably be gone a few more days. You need someone with you. You need someone to help you survive."

She was right. I just hung onto the phone, its strange new weight.

"I'll wear a mask. You can open the windows. There are a lot of ways to die right now and I don't want suicide to be how you go."

I was scared she'd hang up before I said yes, but I couldn't speak.

"Fuck it, Aster. I'm coming over. If you don't let me in, I'll use my key."

✳

I leaned against the door and waited. It seemed to take forever. Every time I thought about what happened I pushed the thought out of my mind and instead remembered watching Mira biting her lip through the peephole. Then she was there again, outside my door. I let her in. She air hugged me without saying a word.

We sat in the living room as it grew dark, then darker.

"Pretend the darkness is a blanket," Mira said. "Pretend it's a lock on your door."

Her words were muffled through her mask. It was cold, but I had all the windows open. Finally I realized we needed to walk Scooby.

"Let's go together," Mira stood up and waited for me to stand up, too. That was how it happened. It wasn't sex at first, just sitting in the dark, just walking the dog, just keeping each other alive through everything that came after. It wasn't love for the longest time, until it was, and then we loved each other so hard it was unbreakable.

Ben never understood why I left him. But she was search and she was rescue.

We lived happily ever after.

FALLING, NOT BREAKING

Annika didn't mean to kill her neighbor. She joked about it with her best friend Sadie, sure, but they joked about a lot of things. Once they texted back-and-forth for over an hour about who they'd cannibalize in the event of the apocalypse. They decided on Sadie's boyfriend Richard, who was meaty and unwilling to take care of himself. Annika's neighbor, Ruthellen, smoked two packs a day and refused to wear a mask. Periodically she left things outside Annika's door—Tupperware, plastic flowers, cards that said HAVE A BUNNY NICE DAY with an Easter bunny surrounded by pastel eggs. The last time Annika had sex was with some random woman she'd met on Tinder. They went to a parking lot. She was exhausted. The pandemic, the rise of fascism, eating her own cooking—it was all too much.

Annika's job was making trailers for new shows on Cat TV, a streaming service exclusively for cats. The trailers weren't for cats, though. They were for people who lived with cats, who bought access to streaming for their cats to watch.

"Why do cats need TV?" Sadie asked. "Can't they look out the window?"

Sometimes Annika felt impatient with this question, which she was asked whenever she talked about her job. The other question people always asked was if she had a cat herself, and if Cat TV was influenced by her personal muse.

"Your meows!" Sadie laughed so loudly she snorted.

Annika did not have a cat. She was a dog person. Annika also had to correct people who clearly thought that she made shows for Cat TV.

"I don't make the shows; I make the trailers for the shows. Like movie trailers for forthcoming films." It got a little confusing, because cats didn't watch the trailers, which were speeded up and compressed, aimed at human attention spans and visual range. Cat TV itself was scientifically formulated to appeal to cats more than any other living creature. It was also rumored to help plants grow, but that was unproven, speculation at best.

Annika made five trailers a week. Usually she made one a day, but occasionally something went wrong and she got backlogged. Then she felt panicky and out of sorts all week. Her job, she knew, impacted the happiness of cats and cat lovers everywhere. It wasn't that making the trailers was difficult. It was that every trailer required actually watching hours of Cat TV, which was incredibly boring, consisting of birds chirping, flying, and sitting on branches;

squirrels gnawing nuts and scurrying up trees; other cats sleeping or licking themselves; and the occasional random nature shot of leaves falling from trees or sunlight on a quiet pond.

Annika had to watch hours and hours of Cat TV, from which she culled highlights of that week's footage, and prepared a trailer of no more than 90 seconds to entice new subscribers to pay $14.99 a month to stream unlimited hours of video content for their extremely pampered, bored apartment cats.

✳

Annika's mother, who was not her best friend but a friend as well as her mother, which made her a rare and precious flower, had called Annika earlier in the week to announce that, first, she had a tumor, and, second, it was wrapped around her head.

"Is it cancer?" Annika asked, because she didn't know what else to say.

"Nope. But it's wrapped around my head."

There was a pause.

"The surgeon says he won't operate."

Another pause. Annika felt panic rising, a flame in her gut, her whole body on fire.

"I'm learning to meditate. I can accept death; I'm 83, and I don't really want to get a lot older."

Annika started to cry silently. Her mother talked about what she'd had for dinner, about her grandkids, and then hung up.

Annika texted Sadie. *My mother has a tumor wrapped around her head.*

Sadie texted back. *I would never cannibalize your mother.*

It was exactly the right thing to say.

✳

Ruthellen wore shapeless pants and applique sweatshirts. She was white in a vague, Republican kind of way. Annika was Swedish. She'd never been to Sweden, but it was where she was from, and she clung to that knowledge. Annika frequently thought about the baby she'd chosen not to have, the abortion she'd had, and wondered if Ruthellen had had abortions, babies, orgasms, sex. According to Marjorie, who lived on the upper floor of Annika's six-plex, Ruthellen spent a lot of time at the casino and was afraid of dying alone and having her body go undiscovered for days. After Annika accidentally killed Ruthellen, she remembered this and felt relieved.

Annika accidentally killed Ruthellen following a muted, polite-yet-ugly altercation that took place primarily over email. The altercation was about Annika's dogs, who barked (according to Ruthellen) whenever Annika left the building. Annika was willing to concede that the dogs barked whenever she left the building, but she never left the building. It was shortly after lockdown began and Annika worked from home. She ordered groceries delivered, exercised 30 minutes a day from 1980's aerobics videos cached online, and spent most of her free time watching reality TV shows on Netflix. She liked the marriage ones, where four couples got married sight unseen and only one couple stayed together. Annika imagined getting married sight unseen, stuffing cake into her gorgeous new wife's mouth, triumphing over the expectations that nonetheless sustained the show.

Ruthellen seemed to believe that Annika left the house frequently, at which point the dogs barked and barked for hours on end. This was not true, Annika explained patiently in full sentences on email, simultaneously texting Sadie *WTF DOES THIS BITCH WANT*

A few days later there was a knock on Annika's door. Immediately both dogs barked uncontrollably. Annika rushed to put on her mask. When she stepped into the hallway, Ruthellen stood less than a foot away, maskless.

Annika froze. Ruthellen began talking but Annika couldn't grasp anything she was saying. Of course it was about the dogs, about noise, and of course the dogs were barking, but mostly Annika kept trying to back away from her maskless neighbor. Ruthellen kept talking, exhaling aerosols, potentially infecting her with every word. The interior hallway of the building was completely enclosed, with a stairway on the right that opened up one story and down another. There was no ventilation. Ruthellen's smoke lingered in the building, commingling with food smells and dog smells and the smells of people living life. Ruthellen talked and talked and then suddenly she was crying. Annika almost reached out an arm to comfort her. She felt terrible. She hadn't been listening, just nodding, shushing the dogs through the door. But now Ruthellen was real to her, a real person who hated noise, as Annika did, too, even though she didn't hate her own dogs' noise. Ruthellen stood lonely and maskless, a white woman in a terrible sweatshirt, crying. Annika hated herself for texting Sadie mean things, for calling Ruthellen a bitch, for saying she would eat Richard. And yet the rage animal inside Annika was still there, would always be there. She was her own guard dog.

✳

That night Annika decided to make apology cookies. She added extra chocolate chips, cinnamon, vanilla, and a little honey. When they were done she put them in the fridge to cool. The next day after work she filled the Tupperware Ruthellen had given her with cookies, gave the dogs treats to quiet them, put on her mask, and walked across the hallway to knock.

"I'm sorry," Annika said when Ruthellen answered her door. "I know the dogs bark. I'm doing my best, but I can do better. Would you like some cookies? Homemade chocolate chip."

Ruthellen was wearing a lilac bathrobe, red slippers, and an orange scarf over her hair. "Would you like to come in?" Annika could see the back of a plaid couch and an overstuffed armchair. She wanted to say yes, but the shared air situation freaked her out. Just then Ruthellen rummaged in the pocket of her bathrobe, pulled out a mask, and put it on. The mask was embroidered with lilacs and matched her bathrobe. It was a good look for Ruthellen.

Annika stepped over the threshold. Smoke hit her in waves, smoke everywhere, ashtrays everywhere. The out-of-controlness of Ruthellen's smoking habit was actually the one thing that made sense to Annika. Everything else in the apartment looked like a stage set for a play about a serial killer, a white lady in her 60's who lured her victims into her apartment by complaining about something—dogs, cats, boyfriends, band practice—only to kill them in some cowardly way that would work both onstage and in the film adaptation. Tidy in the extreme, all the furniture matched, red-and-brown plaid, dark wood furniture, all with the same knobby legs and arms. Two widescreen TVs faced each other on opposite walls, each playing *Fondant or Foxes*.

"My favorite show," Ruthellen pointed to the screen over a display of wide-eyed dolls in pastel lace dresses. They bake cakes and hide them in the forest and contestants have to figure out what's cake and what's real."

Annika nodded, mesmerized by the camera panning slowly through a dark forest. Suddenly hands appeared from out of the frame and grabbed for a rabbit, which turned out to be real. It scampered off through the underbrush while the camera hovered over the contestant's disappointed hands.

"Would you like to see my collection?" Ruthellen gestured toward the kitchen. Annika knew that most serial killers were men, like the guy with the truck whose wife said his victims' ghosts visited her and tipped her off. Still she felt some internal warning, fear or maybe worry, but whether for herself or Ruthellen, she couldn't be sure.

They stepped into the kitchen.

Annika gasped.

All of the cabinets were open-faced, filled with dishes and cups arranged as if in a museum. The colors moved from dark to light on every shelf. Most of the shelves held whole sets of beautiful dishware. Every shelf was labelled with the name of the design.

"This is an amazing collection of dishware," Annika meant it.

"Thank you." Ruthellen smiled and her face relaxed. "It's not that hard. I go to yard sales and estate sales every weekend. You can always come with me if you want. I'll show you what to look for."

Annika shifted from foot to foot, then held out the container of cookies. When Ruthellen hesitated to take one, Annika picked up a cookie and took a bite, in case Ruthellen thought it was impolite to take one first.

"Do they have nuts in them? I'm allergic to peanuts."

"No. I never make them with nuts. There's honey in the batter, though."

"Honey's all right." Ruthellen picked up a cookie and jammed it into her mouth with both hands. Annika forced herself to look away. Ruthellen made a smacking sound. "Good cookie."

Annika folded and unfolded a paper napkin covered in Snoopy cartoons. Childhood felt too close, as if playground bullies might emerge from the bathroom and pull on her hair.

Ruthellen grabbed another cookie and jammed it, whole, into her mouth. Annika didn't know what to do or say. This went on for several cookies. Finally, Annika smiled a forced smile. "Thank you so much for the visit, Ruthellen. You can keep the rest of the cookies. I need to get back to those dogs of mine. It's time for their walk." A lie; she'd walked them an hour ago. Anything to get out of that kitchen.

Annika crumpled her napkin and looked around the room for a trash can. It was on the far end of the room. She walked over, pressed the pedal with her foot, and dropped the crumpled paper into the can. The lid closed slowly, so that Annika could see can after can of Ensure in the bin.

She was trying to think of what to say to Ruthellen, what nice thing that wasn't any version of, "Let's do this again," or "I'll talk with you soon," but was not so rude as, "Your life seems terrible; I can't take it," or "Please, let's try not to cross paths in the hall." Then she heard a thud, as if one of the beautiful dishes had fallen to the floor without breaking, a thud but not a crack, not breaking, just falling. She turned towards the table, but Ruthellen wasn't there.

A slipper. Was that an arm? Annika ran to the overturned chair where Ruthellen lay on the floor, face up. She was gasping, but not really breathing. Her hands were spasming at her throat. Annika pulled down Ruthellen's mask, but it made no difference. They made eye contact.

"I'm sorry. It's okay, it's okay, it's okay. I'm sorry. I'm so sorry, Ruthellen."

Ruthellen stopped breathing. The clock ticked loudly into the silence. Annika tried to think of what she knew of CPR from movies and talking to Richard, who was a nurse. She knelt beside Ruthellen and put one hand tentatively on her chest, then another. Then she thought she should try to dislodge whatever Ruthellen had choked on, and patted her on the back, first tentatively, then harder.

Then Annika realized what she'd done.

She'd made herself a peanut butter sandwich yesterday; was it yesterday or the day before? And wanted honey on the bread. Used the knife, first in the peanut butter, then in the honey, wiping the blade several times on the sticky glass jar to dislodge chunks of peanut butter.

When she'd made the cookies, she'd scooped honey up with a big spoon and hadn't thought twice about it.

Annika realized she needed to call 911. Then she remembered that she had an epi pen in her apartment. She touched Ruthellen's arm even though Ruthellen was unresponsive.

"I'm going to fix this. Don't worry. I'll be right back."

∗

Annika did not go back. She sat in her apartment shaking, curled around first one dog, then the other. She did not, in fact, have an epi pen; she'd used it last time she'd been stung by a bee and her throat started to close. There was danger everywhere. By the time she realized she didn't have one, twenty minutes had passed, and she knew Ruthellen was dead. It made no sense to call 911 to report a death. There was nothing anyone could do.

That night Annika imagined she heard a ghost, first in the hallway, then in her apartment. She imagined Ruthellen's bathrobe hanging from the flagpole outside, where the property management company raised and lowered an American flag every morning. The dogs snored through the night, smelly and warm at her feet, while Annika turned, tossed, and turned again.

The next morning Annika made coffee and let the dogs go out back off leash, something she never did, because it was against the rules. She was in a lawless land. She'd killed someone; now she was letting her dogs run around the building off leash, and when they came back inside she knew she'd stay in her bathrobe all day. She would do things no one ever thought she'd do. Some would be good, some would be bad, and some would be terrible.

The knock on her door startled her. She leaned against the kitchen counter and tried to slow her breathing. Drank the rest of her coffee in one gulp and walked to the door where she stood clutching the floppy sleeves of her bathrobe.

Annika put her eye to the peephole.

In front of her door, fist poised to knock, stood Ruthellen.

She was not a ghost, but a woman in a pink sweatshirt embroidered with kittens tangled in a ball of yarn, wearing a matching pink mask. She held a Tupperware container before her like a shield. It was full of cookies. While Annika watched, Ruthellen set the cookies down in front of her door, walked back to her apartment, and disappeared inside.

TWO

PLACES WE WAIT FOR THE NAMES OF THE DEAD

We wait in the lobby of the Holiday Inn.

We wait in the parking lot outside the Burger King drive-thru.

We wait in the garden behind the Temple.

We wait in the firehouse one block from the school, because the bodies are still inside the school.

Sometimes they mispronounce our dead.

Sometimes we are the dead and we wait also for our names to be called.

When we are the living waiting for the dead, we die in the waiting at the Holiday Inn.

When we are bodies in the school, we are hiding inside the storage closet.

Sometimes they name the shooter before the names of our dead.

Sometimes they name the shooter and he is our son.

When we clean the blood, we wear suits that cover our clothing. When we take off the suits, we have clothes on underneath and we drive home.

Sometimes they make us wait all night. During the night they hold our dead in their arms and turn the bodies carefully for clues. They mark the entrance and exit of the bullets.

When the cameras arrive, they take the last words of the dead.

When we are the dead, we wait by the pool of the hotel.

When we are the dead, we watch the movie again in the empty theater.

When we are the living and we hear the names, we say the names out loud.

We say the names out loud, but no one comes.

We say the names out loud, but no one comes, so we wait in the lobby of the Holiday Inn.

COUP

The coup wasn't why I called my mom. I called my mom because of the global pandemic raging out of control. To make sure she was alive and wasn't coughing. I was walking my dogs in Anacortes, which is sort of a long story and not very interesting. Let's just say it was an unfamiliar town and I called my mom to hear a familiar voice. The voice of love. That's my mom. She answered the call and I was happy to hear her, but the voice of love was frantic. People in red hats were doing what. People were doing what thing now. My mother's voice was clear but nothing she said made sense or anyway I couldn't grasp the thing she said was happening. *Storming* was a word that occurred several times.

I went back to the Airbnb and tried to turn on the television. The remote turned on the heat instead. It was a tiny detached house, probably a garage in The Before Times. They said I could bring my dogs, so I did. The dogs loved it. New smells, a couch made of corduroy they could burrow into. I called my mom back. What she described made less sense than before, but she helped me figure out how to turn on the wide screen TV, the biggest TV I'd ever seen. *Button on the back*, she said. *They're breaking windows! Just press the button. They're attacking police! Can you get CNN? They want to kill Nancy Pelosi!* I pressed everything I could find and finally the screen lit up. I tried to take it all in but there had already been so much outrageousness that more outrageousness wouldn't stick.

My friends kept texting *WTF* and *Are you watching?* I checked my work email because it seemed like maybe there would be an alarm or a bonus for surviving this much Capitalism but instead several colleagues were sending out routine emails, timestamped throughout the day, as if nothing was happening. Maybe they lived in a little bubble like those cat backpacks where a cat sits with their face pressed to the astronaut helmet. It was another one of those traumatic days in US History where something unfathomably terrible happens and then the government goes to war against the will of the people, except this time people were going to war against the government. The people were terrifying. They looked ready to kill. I took the dogs for another walk to try to get away from the wide screen TV which now I could not turn off.

One of the dogs peed on the grass edging the sidewalk outside a white bungalow with green trim. Whoever lived there was on the porch and suddenly they were yelling at me. White dude in a red hat yelling, pointing at a sign: a metal image of a dog, the size of my hands held up in protest. The metal dog was squatting, a tiny metal turd escaping its butt. It was the ugliest art I'd ever seen but he must've liked it. It was right there on his lawn. I wondered how much it cost. I pulled on the dogs' leashes and kept walking. The guy kept yelling. The joke goes: my dogs can't read. That isn't the joke I want to tell. I said, "I'm sorry," because I thought he owned a gun and might shoot me, or worse, shoot my dogs, and then I'd have to kill him, break the windows of his house, stab him with a flagpole. I kept walking until I couldn't hear him yelling anymore.

Later I checked my work email. Everything was operating normally, my ticket to health insurance tied to my ability to answer emails during a coup. I wondered who designed the statue of the pooping dog. If they had health insurance. If they had a dog.

ALTERNATIVE TEACHING MODALITIES IN HELL

Dear Faculty in Hell,

In addition to synchronous, asynchronous, blended, and hybrid online courses, faculty are encouraged to adapt the following face-to-face modalities to promote student retention, community cohesion, and the joyful spirit of learning in hell.

Sincerely,
The Devil, Department of Details

HORSEBACK RIDING (HOR):
All faculty will be assigned to a horse share pool at the start of the semester. Faculty will ride at a canter, weaving past rows of students sitting 6 feet apart on the football field. Using a megaphone (not provided), faculty will lecture by repeating each sentence after every 4 rows of students. Faculty who do not know how to ride a horse may download free tutorials from YouTube.

GIFT BASKETS (GIBETS):
Faculty will prepare a gift basket for each student every week. Suggestions for gift basket items include fresh fruit, gluten-free crackers, vegan jerky, and woodwinds. Inside each gift basket, the week's lectures, assignments, and quizzes will be handwritten on parchment paper. Although faculty will not be compensated for purchasing gift baskets, Home Depot and Cracker Barrel are offering discounts with valid faculty ID.

SHOUTING/SWIMMING (SHOWII):
Faculty will shout important information at students from the shallow end of an open air swimming pool. Students will be encouraged to tread water during the length of the lesson, in which case the course satisfies their physical education requirement. For students who opt not to tread water, a personal floatation device in the form of a wheel (the school's mascot) will

be provided. Faculty who do not know how to swim may download free tutorials from YouTube.

MAGIC (MAC):

While performing magic tricks such as pulling rabbits out of hats and sawing adjuncts in half, tenure-track faculty will invite audience participation in the form of pop quizzes. Students giving wrong answers are invited to disappear in a cloud of smoke.

ONLYFANSFOREDUCATORS (OFFED):

For a limited time, OnlyFans is providing an affiliate service in higher education instruction, available to OnlyFans subscribers at a discounted rate. Although there are currently no for-credit offerings, the university anticipates future partnerships with OnlyFans offering new, self-sustaining degrees in Social Media Marketing and UX Research.

BOOKS (BOKS):

Faculty may suggest that students purchase tangible products, similar to cereal boxes or toilet paper, with printed content inscribed on one or both sides of compressed wood pulp. Students may "borrow" these items and "return" them, using a service called "the library." Faculty who do not know what the library is are encouraged to use Facebook instead.

MEMORANDUM OF UNDERSTANDING REGARDING REPLACEMENTS SHOULD THE WORST OUTCOME OCCUR

Dear Faculty,

We are delighted to inform you of our new policy regarding Teacher Replacements Should The Worst Outcome Occur. Effective immediately, all faculty are invited to name up to three replacements to teach their 2020-2021 courses. Should the worst outcome occur, teachers can die with the comforting knowledge that their courses will continue to meet on Facebook Live.

In naming your replacement, please adhere to the following guidelines:

» Choose someone who is better looking. As peer-reviewed research suggests, the memory of a mediocre thing blends into the memory of a beautiful thing when a mouse is lost in a maze.
» Select someone whose specialty relates to yours but translates better to TikTok.
» Do not choose your office spouse or intellectual rival. Their grief or guilt over your departure may hinder their ability to translate your lectures into entertaining generalizations.
» Post your will on Canvas as a module.
» Learn your students' names and faces in advance, using the confidential photo roster we provide to you without your students' knowledge. Craft an individual goodbye email for each student, making reference to things like academic status ("Junior year is so great!") and photos ("Your hair—it's purple!" "You seem so awake!"). Set the emails on delay, so that each student will receive an email from you when the semester is over. If you aren't dead, you can tell them you were drunk dialing, but on email. They will think this is funny or that you are a fool.
» Do not choose your replacement as punishment for the faculty member least equipped to teach the subject material.
» Do not agree to combine "Rate My Professor" ratings with your replacement.

» If you teach a historically marginalized subject, be sure your replacement is on the same page politically. You can easily determine a colleague's political persuasions by observing their clothing, facial expressions, tone of voice, and coffee mug designs. This is referred to as the "best fit."
» It is not necessary to notify your replacements that you've selected them as replacements. In the event both you and your replacement suffer the worst outcome simultaneously, second-tier replacements will be selected without undue shame or humiliation.
» There will be an award for "Best Performance In the Role of a Replacement" given out to one faculty member during Zoom graduation. If the worst outcome occurs to the awardee before the ceremony, their replacement may take home the statuette.
» Replacements are paid a flat fee of $150 and an unlimited supply of letterhead. Letterhead may be picked up when a vaccine is discovered and administered to everyone on campus. Anti-vaxxers may pick up their letterhead from the Ministry of Supplies at any time.
» Participation by adjunct faculty is encouraged but not required, as adjunct faculty are already treated as replaceable.
» Consider rewriting your will and leaving everything to the Alumni Association. There's still time to ensure that a seat in the stadium will have your name etched on it.

If you have questions regarding these guidelines, please direct them to the Dean of Pandemic Response, Attn: Replacements. Someone will get back to you as their duties permit.

Wishing you an irreplaceable semester,
The Next In Line

DEAR CONSTITUENT,

Thank you for reaching out to express your concern about our recent stock sale. We take the potential to profit from the international public health crisis very seriously. While it is true that last week we sold 50 million dollars in stock which would now be valued at 33 cents, we can assure you that there was no wrongdoing. Our actions are rooted in the values that help make ours one of the biggest pharmaceutical companies in the world. At the core of our value system is our belief that size counts and going big is better than going bankrupt. In order to remain true to our values, we need to remain big. As you probably know, 33 cents is not big, unless you are a small child asking for an allowance or a third ex seeking alimony.

Selling 50 million dollars' worth of stock just before it plunged into an abyss from which it will never recover was entirely coincidental. We don't want to burden you with our personal situation, since this is an entirely professional correspondence sent to you by an automated reply system, but our heir apparent has been in need of a bicycle for a very long time now. Although he is only two (we think), he expresses his wish to ride a very manly sort of bicycle (not a girl's bike) by pedaling his feet in the air when he is throwing a tantrum. We have not observed this behavior firsthand, since he cries a lot and lives in another wing; however, we have heard this repeated by multiple caregivers and, of course, we respect their accounts about as much as we pay them. It would be a terrible thing if our sole acknowledged heir-product went without a bicycle. It was therefore imperative that we liquidate a few of our assets to buy him a top-of-the-line racing bike, akin to those used in the Tour de France and in commercials for anti-depressants where families bicycle together aimlessly, getting lost in the countryside with no cell reception and only a baguette for sustenance.

Of course, we had no knowledge that our stock prices were about to plunge, because we have the greatest faith in our Covid-19 vaccine product, ImpactNah. Our vaccine is unique among the vaccines currently on the market, because it costs almost nothing to produce and is made of nothing. Our vaccine works using the placebo effect, which means there are no side effects or age restrictions. You can get jabbed once, twice, three times. Knock yourself out and get jabbed every day! We don't care what you people are into! Although insurance doesn't cover ImpactNah and the government isn't willing to pay for it, we are confident that over time, the public will come to see the importance of asking for the ImpactNah vaccine by name, even if they've already been vaccinated by a product with all kinds of boring scientific evidence that exhausts us just thinking about it. ImpactNah works differently, because it doesn't work at all. By harnessing the healing powers of the imagination, our vaccine triggers a powerful burst of faith in Big Pharma and for-profit medicine, leading our patients' bodies to tingle and feel hopeful for the first time in years. That burst of hope helps the body fight Covid-19 in an imaginary, fun kind of way. $400 out-of-pocket is a small price to pay for peace of mind with no scientific basis and a 0% efficacy rating, based on injecting close friends and family members with nothing and asking them how they felt.

Now, if you'll forgive us, we have a gender reveal party/paternity suit/offshore drilling event to attend. This is why we will be unable to answer texts, emails, phone calls, faxes, DMs, Craigslist missed connections, TikTok challenges, or knocking on heaven's door for the foreseeable future.

Enjoy your life post-vaccination and remember, it's probably going to be short!

Sincerely,
Do Not Reply

FIELD

I was not in a restaurant because the restaurants were closed, except for the restaurants which were open. Maskless people sat at tables, breathing, waiting for servers, who were wearing masks. The servers looked like nurses in plastic face shields and gloves. I was not in Canada because the border was closed. I was not at work because I worked remotely, which happened suddenly: I received an email at 11pm and began working remotely at 8 the next morning. I was not in my car. I was not on my sofa. I was not at my best friend's house watching TV.

I was in a field, except not really a field, but the space between rows of identical houses, where more rows of identical houses would soon be built. I found the field on accident when I strayed off path. Nothing was happening there, and nothing would happen there for maybe a year, but it was circled with temporary fencing and orange tarp. For the longest time when I looked at the fencing, I saw a space that said Keep Out. I was on one side of the fence and the field was on the other. The fence and the tarp meant Do Not Cross. Then one day the big dog ran up to the fence and tried to slip under to chase a rabbit or maybe a bird. He also chased cars and after I first adopted him I doubted my ability to keep him alive. Then I noticed a gap between two fence posts and slipped in with both dogs on leash. From inside the fence I realized that it wasn't keeping me out so much as designating the space where ground would soon be broken.

No one cared that I was in the field. They saw only the space between houses, the money that had gone into clearing the space, the money it would take to build. The field was a place to let the dogs off leash and not have to wrangle their feral instincts as we walked on narrow sidewalks where people also walked. I could stare off into the distance, which included a farm and a golf course and also woods. Coyote hunted in the brush, sometimes roaming into town. The view was campestral, both wild and tame. I had to be careful. If I looked too far past what I knew, a hawk might swoop down over the small dog, who mostly clung to my ankles. I knew I wouldn't let it happen, but I also knew I didn't know much. Farther off, on the green grass of the golf course, white people walked around a manmade lake. The weather was perfect, meaning it wasn't anything. I look off my mask. The dogs ran until they couldn't run.

Q&A

Sometimes I lose myself washing my hands. Look up from the sink to find skin rubbed raw. Sometimes I walk the overgrown coil of the greenspace that buffers the Burlington Northern. I tell myself the houses are moving. I say trains stand still while we whistle away.

∗

You told me while we were walking the dog. "I'm in love," you said, and I thought you meant me. Then I thought you meant oranges, Velcro, or earthquakes. But her name was WHATEVER. And pretty, you said.

You wanted, you said, one night a week. The day of the night and the after day, too. So many days in a marriage, you said. It was something for you after too much of mine.

Gone Thursday morning. Home Friday night.

∗

My job was words, lining them up. I wrote scripts for a personal voice recognition system. My job was to come up with questions. When I first started, I kept trying to hand in questions and answers. It seemed reasonable they'd be a package deal.

My boss shook his head.

"You're Questions," he said, slurping the last of his liquid meal through a metal straw. He jogged in place at his treadmill desk. "Let Answers answer the questions. You're Questions. It's a good place to be."

"Why good?"

"Because answers go wrong. It's the answering part where people get mad."

After that I gave up and stuck to the script, asking questions that would allow a machine to answer with as much accuracy as a human being. Script writers worked backwards. I wrote questions, someone else wrote answers, and out of the combination, someone else wrote commands. The current category was *Transportation*. In anticipation of civilian space travel, I had to come up with questions for IRL aerospace events. Subheadings included *urination in space* and *giving consent in Zero G*.

Like everyone else in tech I was on a spin cycle of anxiety about whether my job had any meaning at all, whether it was good or evil or morally neutral. My five minute breaks vanished quickly, timer on my laptop ticking down the seconds. Everyone at work used Pomodoros, but no one was on the same cycle. People took breaks at erratic times. Management was just part of people, so we were always off tempo, unable to sync.

*

The first Thursday night I trimmed my hair. Soft sound of falling, spent cells on the floor. Furred fringe of bangs in a clear plastic bag. Dog chasing leaves, unbuckling dead things.

Then the basement filled with water. I learned to live with it, as I lived with everything else. Our flooded house was across from a park, children on leash and dogs on display. Sometimes the curtains in our windows were yellow and sometimes the curtains in our windows were blue. The only green thing was the flood in our basement, cool like your eyes, shifting each day.

EPISTEMOLOGY

The moment before the moment you knew.

The moment you knew.

The moment you stood in the knowing.

The moment after the moment you knew.

The moment after the moment you knew before you knew what you know now.

The moment you erased the knowing.

The moment you stood in not knowing again.

The moment after erasing the knowing when you stood in the room and opened the door. The moment you saw the person you knew.

The moment erasing became what you knew.

The moment you laughed and had dinner, not knowing.

The moment erasing the knowing stopped working.

The moment before the moment you knew again the thing you'd stopped knowing before. The moment you walked through the door in your knowing.

The moment your knowing became what you knew.

The moment of facing the person who knew the knowing you knew, but not your knowing.

The moment of naming.

The person erasing.

The moment of knowing erasing was naming.

The moment you shut the door on not knowing.

The moment a stranger knocked on your door.

ANTI-BODY

My Antibodies and I lounge in bed on Saturday morning. Already we're inseparable.

"I know this is new," I say, "but it feels really good."

We get out of bed.

We get dressed.

We're wearing the same clothes!

We're in the same body!

They tell me their relationships only last six months, but they've been working on this in therapy.

"Maybe a six month check in. Just to be sure."

I try not to let this scare me. They want to take me to a restaurant, but it feels like too much, too soon. It's enough just to sit in a room together and watch TV.

"I've been in survival mode for a year," I tell them. "It's hard to believe you're real."

My arm itches, a bite from the first time we touched.

I don't ask them if they're seeing other people. I know the answer will be yes.

FAIRY TALE POST-QUARANTINE EMPLOYEE REENTRY

Once upon a time there was a terrible King.

✳

Every door has been rekeyed. Every lock takes a different key. Every key is a different shape and hangs from your hip on a chain that clatters when you walk down the windowless hall in search of gold coins.

✳

"What is this red and curious stain on the carpet? Could it be wine, tea, or the blood of an unsuccessful suitor?"

✳

You live with a wolf that has grown strangely attached. When you leave the wolf alone for the first time, it howls nonstop and your neighbors hurl curses.

✳

As you open the door and step into blinding sunlight, you see fires in the distance. Smoke smothers the hills. The maps are all outdated. You walk and walk, but everything remains as far away as before.

✳

Buildings have fallen into decay. Strangers pass silently, six feet apart.

✳

No one remembers your name. Or was your name always *Handmaid, Woodsman, Witch?*

✳

Sourdough breadcrumbs lead to a house in the woods. The house is made of candy and tastes like the fear of being followed.

✳

Everything is frozen in time, exactly as it was, except for the beanstalk growing from a can of coffee.

✳

You are given three tasks. After each task, you must stand in front of the Higher Ups and avert your eyes as they judge your prowess. With every failure, your circumstances become more dire.

✳

The ring glows just out of reach.

✳

Your boss drives a pumpkin-colored carriage and parks defiantly in the "No Parking" zone.

✳

The costumes at the masked ball keep changing. Everyone takes off their masks, puts them on again, removes them. The crowd's a sea of gaping mouths, white teeth gleaming.

✳

Your coworker seems to be sleeping, eyes closed, hands folded on her chest, her face serene under the glass ceiling, so of course some guy kisses her without her consent.

✳

At night you toss and turn, unable to sleep, as if there's a lump in your mattress or a lump in your throat.

✳

Trigger warning: the deaths in these stories will haunt you.

✳

You sense danger at every turn.

FOXES: A PLAY IN ONE ACT

CAST OF CHARACTERS
    Dahlia Lark: a woman in her sixties, married to Ransom.
    Ransom Lark: a man in his sixties, married to Dahlia.
    Max: a plumber, any gender, any age.
    Four: a young woman.
    Hound: a personal assistant voice recognition system.

SETTING
    In the kitchen of the Lark house.

Dahlia is cleaning the kitchen. There's a knock on the door. Dahlia opens the door and Max steps inside.

Max	You buried.
Dahlia	Three cats.
Max	And a dog?
Dahlia	Gone missing.
Max	We'll be back in the morning.
Dahlia	Did you find.
Max	Not yet.
Dahlia	Thank you, Max.
Max	You're welcome, Mrs. Lark. *Shuts door.*

Dahlia returns to cleaning the kitchen. Turns on the tap, listens for water. Begins washing dishes. Ransom enters. Opens the refrigerator, takes out a beer. Sits at the kitchen table and drinks.

Dahlia	How was your day?
Ransom	Same as always.
Dahlia	I'm sure something happened. Something big, something small, could be anything, really.
Ransom	Nothing happened today.
Dahlia	Did you sell any?
Ransom	One.
Dahlia	That's good. That's great! You sold one. You did! Would you like chicken or fish?
Ransom	What kind of fish?
Dahlia	The chicken's just chicken and the fish is trout.

Ransom Trout.

Dahlia Would you like potatoes?

Ransom Yes. And the orange.

Dahlia Carrots! I knew you'd like them. Like eating chips but they aren't chips. They're so good for you. They have vitamin A.

Ransom Who was that?

Dahlia No one. I didn't see anyone.

Ransom In the driveway just now.

Dahlia That was the plumber. The pipes clogged last week while you were away.

Ransom You should ask me to fix things.

Dahlia I didn't want you to worry.

Ransom Strangers can't give you anything you need.

Ransom's phone begins to vibrate. They both stare at the phone.

Ransom I have to go. Put my plate in the fridge.

Dahlia But you just got home and it's after six.

Ransom Sweetheart, relax. Watch one of your shows.

Dahlia What time will you.

Ransom Time's not for you to decide. *Exits.*

Dahlia watches him leave. Paces around the kitchen, picks up a bag of candy. Turns on the TV and sits with the bag. Begins watching TV and eating candy, throwing wrappers on the floor. Four enters through the front door. Begins picking up candy wrappers. Smooths them out, puts them on the counter. Opens the refrigerator door, takes out a beer, pops the top. Doesn't drink.

Dahlia *Startled by the noise.* Like a gun going off.

Four freezes while Dahlia gets up and looks around the kitchen. Four moves to avoid being seen. Dahlia sits back down. Four opens the refrigerator and pops the top of another beer. Dahlia gets up slowly, turns around to see Four.

Dahlia The door–

Four Unlocked.

Dahlia You live–

Four Out back.

Dahlia I thought–

Four For years.

70

Dahlia	I thought I was alone.
Four	You can see from your window.
Dahlia	A deer caught in headlights.
Four	The gaze braced for impact.
Dahlia	There was always so much.
Four	Let's not. *Stares at the television.* What are you watching?
Dahlia	My baking show. They bake cakes in the shape of flowers and moss and pinecones and birds and deer and rabbits and antlers. They bake cakes and hide them in the forest and contestants have to figure out what's cake and what's real. This is season three. It's called *Fondant or Foxes.*
Four	I've never seen–
Dahlia	Well, you wouldn't have, would you? I'm sorry. I'm so sorry.
Four	May I have a glass of water? I just want something to hold.

Dahlia brings Four a glass of water. Four looks at the glass, turning it around. Doesn't drink.

Four	Trouble with the pipes?
Dahlia	Probably roots. Starting tomorrow they're digging the yard.
Four	Mrs. Lark.
Dahlia	Call me Dahlia. Your name?
Four	Four.
Dahlia	I drove past you on the side of the road.
Four	That wasn't me.
Dahlia	She looked just like you.
Four	That was probably Six. We look sort of alike.
Dahlia	Why did he pick you?
Four	We all had hands. Our eyes looked out. Why did he pick you?
Dahlia	We met in church. He had a beautiful voice and all I could do was listen. I wasn't the prettiest or the smartest. I was just a girl in the choir.
Four	Sometimes the others–
Dahlia	The others? Out back?
Four	Sometimes at night we talk about why.
Dahlia	He picked you; you were special to him. He picked me because I wasn't special.
Four	I would've picked you.
Dahlia	I'm not like that.

Four	How do you know if you're always for him?
Dahlia	If you weren't the girl on the side of the road.
Four	I worked in the library. She was a waitress.
Dahlia	It's not like he made a list.
Four	He makes lots of lists. There's one right here. *Pulls a scrap of paper out of the Bible.*

Dahlia leans over Four's shoulder. They read silently, then Four puts the paper back in the Bible.

Dahlia	Thank you for stopping by. It's been a delightful visit. I appreciate you! Thank you! I want to watch my show now.
Four	*Opens the refrigerator door.* Poor chicken.
Dahlia	Please leave.
Four	Excuse me?
Dahlia	This is my house and I did not invite you. If you don't leave, I'll call the police.
Four	That sounds like a great idea.
Dahlia	I said go and you're still here.
Four	I'm only here because you're seeing me.
Dahlia	I have to finish my show.
Four	I'm not stopping you.
Dahlia	I have to find out if the bird's nest is real.
Four	Dahlia, listen to me very carefully.
Dahlia	*Covers her ears.* I don't need to listen to a thing you say.
Four	No, you don't. You already know.
Dahlia	You aren't even real. You're just a comb in a box.
Four	So you know about the boxes.
Dahlia	I'm making you up. *Hits herself.* I just need to stop.
Four	Dahlia, listen to me very carefully. He's got a girl in the front seat of his car.
Dahlia	Ransom works late. Sometimes husbands do.
Four	She's working, too. She'll try to hang on. She'll roll down the window, blow smoke at the trees.
Dahlia	This is my house and you need to go.
Four	You haven't asked me why I'm here.
Dahlia	Why are you here, then?
Four	You have to stop him.
Dahlia	You're uninvited.
Four	I've lived here for years. It's not about you. It's about us. We're all out back. They won't find us whole.
Dahlia	You're asking me to risk.

Four	No, Dahlia. The risk is the lie you tell if you stay.
Dahlia	When did you know?
Four	Not right away.
Dahlia	Was he wearing his–
Four	No.
Dahlia	Did you know he was–
Four	He was good looking and I wanted a ride.

Someone knocks on the front door. Four goes into the bedroom. Someone knocks on the front door again. Dahlia looks through the peephole, then opens the door for Max.

Max	Sorry to bother you, Mrs. Lark.
Dahlia	Call me Dahlia. Please come in.
Max	We were covering one of the pipes with tarp and picked up a rock to pin it down. We found something. Under the rock.
Dahlia	You found…
Max	A watch. Thought you might want it. *Hands her the watch.*
Dahlia	Thank you, Max.
Max	You're welcome, Dahlia.

Max exits. Four enters a moment later. Grabs the watch.

Four	That's mine.
Dahlia	It's nice.
Four	It's cracked and it's bitten and there's blood on the band.
Dahlia	But what a clever design, the hands shaped like–
Four	Really?
Dahlia	I mean, you have lovely style. You just wanted nice things.
Four	I stole it. *Pause.* Just kidding. He bought it for me.
Dahlia	You're talking about my husband.
Four	We went to a drug store because he wanted cigarettes and I saw the watch and liked it and he bought it for me.
Dahlia	That doesn't make sense. Ransom doesn't smoke.
Four	He smoked plenty with me.
Dahlia	I don't believe you.
Four	Dahlia, listen. They're going to find things.
Dahlia	What kinds of things?
Four	Barrettes. Shoes. A ring.
Dahlia	A ring?
Four	She was married.
Dahlia	Which one?

Four	Three.
Dahlia	Did her husband?
Four	Her wife.
Dahlia	Once he caught me with a cigarette. He caught me and–
Four	His eyes changed.
Dahlia	The way he looked at me scared me.
Four	You're his secret.
Dahlia	I'm his wife.
Four	It all depends on who comes home safe.
Dahlia	Ransom is a good husband. We have a beautiful home.
Four	He made it sound like he was single. Just wanted a girl, a beer, some fun.
Dahlia	He likes me clean.
Four	Dead doesn't mean dirty.
Dahlia	This is my house.
Four	I sleep here, too. Look, Dahlia. They're fixing the sewer. They're fixing the sewer by digging the yard. It's only a matter of time before they start to find.
Dahlia	I don't understand what you want from me.
Four	Tell someone the truth. Someone you trust. You won't be more alone than you are now.
Dahlia	What if he finds–
Four	Drive into town. Or just keep driving.
Dahlia	Ransom would never hurt me.
Four	This isn't about what you think he'd do.
Dahlia	I don't have words.
Four	Find them, quick.
Dahlia.	*Paces. Picks up the phone, puts it down.* What if. What do I say. *Taps out a number, pauses, stops. Taps out a number again.* Hello? Yes. This is Dahlia Lark. I live at 819 Briar Ridge Court. The usual. That's right. *Hangs up.*
Four	You called.
Dahlia	I said–
Four	You ordered pizza.
Dahlia	I'm hungry. Do you want to eat.
Four	I can't.
Dahlia	Of course.
Four	You have to save her. By now he has her in the back of his car.
Dahlia	I think you should go.
Four	You can't unsee me.

Dahlia	You're making things up.
Four	You're talking to me.
Dahlia	I have to think of my marriage. My husband. Our home. Ransom works too hard, but he does it for me.
Four	How did your dog die?
Dahlia	Ransom would never.
Four	What did he tell you.
Dahlia	In the woods, hunting. It was an accident. Our dog slipped away. Out past the trees.
Four	That's not what happened.
Dahlia	A gold blur in the pines.
Four	We were in a ravine. Me and your husband. Your dog saw Ransom with his hands on me and turned on him. Your dog turned on your husband. Tried to save me. That's what your dog did.
Dahlia	Ransom would never.
Four	Ransom just drove off. Left me and your dog in the ravine to die.
Dahlia	Did someone find–
Four	You get one happy ending. Your dog's not dead. Someone good picked him up.
Dahlia	I have to find Teddy.
Four	Leave your dog where he is. He's better off gone when Ransom comes home.
Dahlia	How long until…
Four	It depends on how quickly.
Dahlia	It's not like I don't see things. I do. It was cold, I think early December. He said he'd gone hunting. His pants caked with mud.
Four	And he drove…
Dahlia	Past the garage.
Four	You watched from the bedroom.
Dahlia	Something in boxes.
Four	You're just the one he decided to keep.
Dahlia	This is my husband you're talking about.
Four	Your husband whose hands–
Dahlia	We got married in church.
Four	What does your god say?
Dahlia	It's not about God.
Four	Does he know who you are? I mean, really know you.
Dahlia	God or my husband?
Four	Aren't they the same?

Dahlia	He knows things. There are things I keep hidden.
Four	What would he say if he knew what you did?
Dahlia	What I...
Four	I know everything. *Bursts out laughing.* Okay, that's from a movie. It's not really like that, but I know you've got secrets because everyone does.
Dahlia	What I–
Four	You think because you're keeping secrets that you have to let him have his own. But your secrets aren't the same, Dahlia. One lie isn't the same as the next.
Dahlia	I'm making you up.
Four	Would you really invent this?
Dahlia	Maybe I'm drunk and don't remember the wine. You're not real. I'm twisting nightmares to knots.
Four	Let's think this through. If you're right, and I'm not here, and you're drunk, imagining horrible things, what's the worst that could happen?
Dahlia	My husband comes home.
Four	And if I'm here and it's true?
Dahlia	My husband comes home.
Four	Ransom told you Teddy was dead.
Dahlia	Sometimes husbands are wrong. It doesn't mean they're evil or do terrible things.
Four	Pick up the phone.
Dahlia	Should I call 911? Maybe the library. What would you do?
Four	What I would do isn't much help. *Claps hands.* Hound, let's go.
Hound	How can I help you?
Four	Hound, please Google, "Who to call to report that your husband is a serial killer."
Hound	In the United States or Internationally?
Dahlia	Who's that? Where's that voice coming from?
Four	*Points to glowing box.* It's Hound. I noticed you had one. Is it always turned on? Is it recording?

Dahlia walks over to the box, touches it. Sputtering sound turns into the sound of a car in traffic.

Four	What does that sound like to you?
Dahlia	It sounds like traffic.
Four	From inside a car.
Dahlia	Maybe it's the radio. Books-on-tape.

Four	That's the sound of tracking. There's a recording device inside his car.
Dahlia	Don't be ridiculous. How would.
Four	You should know.
Dahlia	I don't.
Four	Remember.
Dahlia	No.
Four	You don't remember putting a recording device inside your husband's car?

Traffic noise shifts slightly. Other noises filter in.

Four	Listen.
Dahlia	Gravel.
Four	He's turning off the main road. The road's unpaved.
Dahlia	Hunting. It's a hobby, it's how he relaxes, it's.
Four	I thought he was with a client, working late tonight.
Dahlia	Maybe the client didn't show up, maybe he went hunting instead. His yellow vest, shotgun, white tail through trees.
Four	Hunting. At night.
Dahlia	He knows how to aim.
Four	Does he see in the dark?

The car noise shifts again. There's a pause, then a door opens and shuts. Footsteps crunch on gravel.

Dahlia	Turn it off.
Four	I can't.
Dahlia	Make it stop.
Four	He's your husband.
Dahlia	*Claps hands.* Hound, stop.

The noise stops.

Four	So you know what to do.
Dahlia	Why are you looking at me like that?
Four	I'm just waiting. Time's on my side.
Dahlia	You're very perceptive, you're lovely, thank you for coming over tonight. Now go back to wherever you came from.
Four	I live here. In your backyard.
Dahlia	What if it's you?
Four	What do you mean?

Dahlia   What if you did terrible things and you've broken into
         my house and now you're trying to turn me against
         my husband?
Four   *Claps hands.* Hound, let's go.

*Staticky noises that slowly turn to the sound of a forest. Underneath this
sound, very faint, are voices, too low and faraway to make out any words.*

Dahlia   *Claps hands.* Hound, stop.
Four   You have to trust me.
Dahlia   That's what Ransom says.
Four   You're in control now. You're tracking him. You're
         recording all of it and you'll have evidence.
Dahlia   *Claps hands.* Hound, let's go.

Sound of static, sputtering, then voices, faint and far away.

Four   *Claps hands.* Hound, stop.
Dahlia   Why did you...
Four   I know what comes next.

Sound of a car in the driveway, startling them both.

Four   This wasn't part of the plan.

Four exits.

Dahlia   Who is it?

Sound of a car driving away. Then a dog, barking.

THREE

THINGS WE TOUCHED INSTEAD OF SKIN

I knock on the wrong door. You're not behind the door, but inside a house you built with your hands. Inside the house, you sit at a table with your wife and daughter. Dinner grows cold, forks and spoons shivering against plant matter piled on plates. I stop knocking when my knuckles redden. I walk past the window where you light the room.

✳

I met your wife first. She was talking about divorce. How easy it was because you made it so. How you asked for nothing when she said she was leaving. How you made things so nice while she did as she pleased. She took tiny jars out of a paper bag and set them on the table in rows and rows, every jar a different color. Then other things she kept in the bag, and then she layered everything and made some sort of a cake. She wasn't really talking to me, but she wasn't not talking to me at this party. She put the layered stuff on plates. It wasn't my house. It wasn't hers, either.

I watched as someone entered the room, late to the party, a pause in the doorway. The party got hotter. Everyone spilled outside around a fire. You were keeping a lawn chair from leaving by sitting on its very edge. I walked up to the chair beside you and touched its cold shoulder.

✳

I imagine you imagining me. This game is better than imagining you, because I know you; I don't need to imagine. In my head we're on my sofa again, in the apartment on the busy street. When I moved out, I took a photo of the empty room and sent it to you. You knew what it meant. The first time you came to my apartment, someone let you in the security doors, so you knocked on my door without me buzzing you in. I looked through the peephole. You had on a hoodie and you were shifting from foot to foot, like your voice might spill if you stood still. My neighbors had security cameras all up and down the front of their door, pointed at you, my door, and my peephole. I let you in quickly. We both knew the story: what happens when someone with dark skin in a hoodie knocks on a door with a white woman inside.

✳

We sat on my sofa for the longest time, not speaking. This was how it started. It didn't start with touch or even words, but what we felt when those things drained away. You didn't look at me the way I wanted you to, but neither did you look at anyone else. I wasn't sure what you wanted, if it was me, or someone different from me, different parts or skin or gestures. We talked about books. How we wished things were different. Other planets, places to fly. The stillness when you looked me right in the eye was the same stillness I'd felt that first night at the party. Everything stopped. I wanted to do that for you.

✳

You wife doesn't want you but won't let you go. She wants a divorce, but she wants you to miss her. You've never lived without each other. She tells you to move into the basement, so you do. Your daughter goes up and down the stairs fifteen times a day, as if this is normal, as if nothing has changed. Your wife places an ad on Tinder. You make small talk all day, eat dinner together. You give up on the things you both promised but stay trapped together by the things you can't say.

✳

One day you tell your wife that there's something between us. A door opens in the conversation. You walk through the door; she closes the door. I want to say, *I will break down the door for you,* but in any context, that is not what I mean. What I mean is, I climbed through your window and found myself standing in front of you, glass around our feet. We knew we had to move carefully. One misstep and someone would bleed. At the far end of the room full of broken glass was a bed. We each had to make our own way through the maze, shards glinting in the hope we'd be held.

✳

Sickness coats my throat and I recede into rashes and raspy breathing. No one touches anyone in this town.
We cover our mouths.

We pass on the street and don't look back.

*

There's something outside the door to your house, fluttering. It might be the sickness, but it might be a bird. If it's the sickness and you move out, you'll die. If it's a bird, you'll discover that you're also a bird. You'll fly away with the others. You'll return every Spring. You'll watch over your daughter from a perch in the trees.

THE VACCINE KID

The kid said he had the vaccine in the freezer. The kid said he could fly, said his dad wasn't his dad, said his mom was really his sister. Said he was an animal in the skin of a human child. Said he had a million dollars under his mattress.

"More like twenty bucks," I lifted the mattress and pointed at the pile of crumpled ones and candy wrappers. I stopped laughing when he kicked me. The kid was twelve or thirteen, tops.

"Shut the fuck up, Millennial."

"I'm not a millennial."

"Boomer."

"I'm Gen X and you need to stop kicking. It hurts."

The kid was related to me, but we didn't really know each other. He was my second cousin's kid. I didn't know my second cousin, either. Everyone in my bio family got sick at once and suddenly I had this kid. I drove from Seattle to Birch Bay to take care of him. Birch Bay sounded like a resort but when I got there the water was red tide for days and the waterslides were closed, not just because of the pandemic, but because they were made out of matchsticks and halfway unmoored. There was a burger joint that was open for takeout, and a bar filled with maskless people risking it all for a beer and a light. The candy shop had milkshakes and every kind of sweet you could imagine. If you walked along the beach and looked past the dead fish and tainted seaweed, the bay was gold in sunlight, silver in rain.

How the kid's family ended up in Birch Bay wasn't clear to me. Something about being close to the border. But now the border was closed, and everyone was trapped on the American side while Trudeau ran his hands through his hair like a boss.

I made the kid wear a mask around me for the first few days.

"C'mon, kid," I said, when he pulled it down to his chin. I could see the aerosols, kid-spittle and disease hanging between us. If he had it, now I had it, too. Eventually I gave up and took off my mask in the house, which was a condo facing away from the water.

The kid's name was Samuel, but everyone called him Milky, because one year when he was small he'd taken a pitcher of milk and poured it over his head. I wasn't there. I was never there. I was the one who escaped the family. But now here I was, with a kid, in a condo that faced away from a stinking red tide. Now here I was, shopping for two at the only grocery store, which was sort of like a 7-11.

"We're gonna eat frozen burritos forever."

"You got a problem with that, my dude?"

That first night, though, I made spaghetti with sauce I cooked myself: tomatoes, garlic, basil, and onions I browned in a pan. Milky was impressed, I could tell. He twirled spaghetti on his fork and slurped.

"Are my parents going to die?"

"I thought you said they weren't your parents," I almost snapped, stopping myself just in time. That was the old me, the way I was before the pandemic. Edgy. My parents threw me in a pool when I three was to see if I could swim. Like a witch, I bobbed along the water. I don't remember applause or even a towel. Survival was its own reward. Nurturing wasn't a thing that I did, not knowing where to keep it in a chest like mine.

But now everything around me had changed and change demanded that I change, too.

I shook my head and tried to look confident. "Your parents are going to be fine," I lied.

"How come they picked you to take care of me instead of somebody more like a mom?"

"Maybe they wanted a bad influence."

Milky snorted. I hadn't meant to be funny; it was just true. Everyone knew I was the baddie, the one who left. The one who didn't send gifts on holidays or birthdays. The one with opinions. Out on my own.

"The one who has a life," my partner Kate said whenever I felt guilty, which wasn't often. I wondered if Milky knew I was the gay one. Kate had stayed in Seattle with the dogs and the pod. The idea was that I'd take care of Milky for two weeks, then head back to Seattle and quarantine for another two weeks before re-joining the household. No one in the pod was happy about it, least of all me. But what could I say?

"He's a kid and both his parents are in the fucking ICU."

Kate, Lina, and Richard exchanged glances.

"Look, Sadie," Richard sighed. "It's just that we worked so hard to sync up the polycule into a pandemic pod."

I burst out laughing. It sounded ridiculous, even though it was honest. Everyone had quarantined in separate rooms for two weeks, then all four of us had gotten Covid tested on the same day. Kate and Lina still sometimes wore masks around Richard, who was a nurse and swabbed noses all day. I understood their caution, but it also felt biphobic, since Kate was lesbian in that old school way and resented my relationship with Richard from the start.

"We're partners. We're poly. You have a girlfriend; I have a boyfriend. Everyone gets along. What's the problem?"

She couldn't explain; when she tried, it was so based in outdated stereotypes about biology and gender that I felt like I was talking to my right-wing Republican parents.

Still, I missed Kate something fierce. We'd promised to talk every night and text all the time, but I could see already that Milky was going to be a bigger job than I'd thought.

"It's okay if you don't text me twice a day, but you can't text Richard then, either."

I never texted Richard. "Sounds good."

That night Milky and I split a pint of ice cream and watched reality TV. I wanted to watch the real estate one and he wanted to watch the wilderness one, so we compromised and watched the baking one, only not the one where people made proper pastries under a great white tent, but the one where the cakes looked like pinecones and moss. Bakers hid cakes in the forest and contestants had to figure out what was cake and what was real. It was satisfying to watch the camera pan through the woods, to feel content eating ice cream from the pint with two spoons.

That night I dreamed about car alarms and jackhammers. I dreamed that I clomped through a library in squeaky rain boots and a row of librarians stood up to say, "Shush!"

I woke up to a series of confusing texts from my sister; my phone had been beeping alerts all night long. The good news was that my cousins were going to make it. They'd both turned a corner; now they were out of the ICU and in the regular part of the hospital. Breathing on their own, just resting. Recovering until they were strong enough to come home.

The confusing part was that Milky was recovering, too.

I texted my sister back, thinking maybe I'd misinterpreted her emojis and exclamation marks.

Can you explain what you said about Milky?
Sadie he IS going to BE OK!!!!!! ☺
Okay how?
Breathing LIKE A MAN. He will COME HOME SOON!!!!! ☺

Something told me I shouldn't text her back, telling her I knew Milky was fine because he was right here with me, eating ice cream and watching bad baking, walking on the boardwalk, looking out at the red tide.

My sister and I hadn't spoken since I saw she had both *Trump 2024* and *MAGA* bumper stickers on her SUV. The last thing she'd said to me was that I needed Botox if I was ever going to find a husband.

It was up to me to solve the Mystery of Milky.

For starters, I thought I'd ask Milky himself.

"Hey, Milky!"

"Whuzzup, Gen X?"

"Who are you really, my dude?"

"I'm just me. Who the hell are you?"

"I'm Sadie, and you're a liar."

He got quiet. Looked down at his shoes. Then he jumped off the couch and made a break for the door. I watched him race to the door, rush outside, slam the door behind him, open it again, shut the door, and sit back down on the couch like he had nowhere else to go.

I walked into the kitchen. Shook a bag of chips into a bowl. Put a burrito in the microwave and poured him a soda, the kind I was always telling him he shouldn't drink.

When I got back to the living room he was still there, so quiet and sunken he belonged to the couch.

"What's your name?"

He shook his head.

"Want an easier question?"

He nodded.

"Do you even know my cousins?"

"Milky's my friend."

That made sense.

"Is Milky going to be okay?"

"Sure thing. They all are. Have some chips before I eat them first."

He put two chips in his mouth at once, out the sides like fangs. "Maybe I'm a vampire."

"Maybe you are."

"Aren't you scared of me?"

"Not even a little. Where are your parents?"

"I left them at the store."

"So you ran away?"

"I just didn't go home."

"Kid, whoever you are, look. I've gotta take you back to your family. I could be accused of child-napping. Of stealing a human person."

"Don't worry. No one's coming for me."

It hurt, how he said it. I believed him. "What's your real name?"

"Conjunctivitis."

I groaned.

"Hans Solo."

"C'mon, kid. You can tell me."

He got quiet. We sat in stillness. Finally I reached over and put two chips in my mouth like fangs.

"What's your name? For real."

"I can't tell you."

"Try me." I crunched the chips. "I'm still here. I'm not going away."

"Promise you won't hurt me."

I felt something well up inside. "Nobody's going to hurt you, I promise. You're safe with me."

"Jennifer."

I didn't want to say the wrong thing, so I said nothing. The kid said nothing, too, so finally I asked, "What would you rather be called?"

That was how Jack became Jack. We went down to the red tide. I carried a bottle of water and we stood as close to the tide as we could without touching. Then I poured the water over Jack's head.

"You're Jack now."

"No more Jennifer?"

"No more of that nonsense."

"Are you gonna take me back to my parents? They won't let me be Jack. They'll make me wear dresses again. At church they'll pray for me and say they'll send me away to some camp."

"Jack, I need you to listen. This is important. I need you to tell me the truth. What really happened to Samuel and his parents?"

"Can we just walk?"

We walked along the beach until we got to the sweet shop. Then I went in and got us each a bag of candy, licorice for me and gummy worms for Jack. When I came out of the store, he wasn't there. Instead I saw a big family standing by their car, reading a map. None of them wore masks. I felt sick and wondered if they were Jack's family and they'd stuffed him in the trunk of their car. But then he wandered over from the side of the building and we took our candy and walked away.

When we got to a bench I sat down and patted the space beside me. Jack didn't sit down, but he didn't leave, either. He stared out over the water for the longest time.

"My family was staying a few doors down and I went swimming with Samuel every morning. Then one morning I knocked, and no one answered. It was the same every morning for a few days. I don't remember everything. But one day I realized the door was open just a little. So I pushed it with my shoulder and went in and they were all really sick. I called 911 and an ambulance came. I didn't mean to lie, but when they asked who I was I said Samuel's brother. They wanted to take me to the hospital, but I said I'd stick around and call relatives. Tell everyone what happened. And someone was supposed to come get me, but they just forgot, I guess. Since Samuel didn't have an actual brother it's not like someone was looking for me."

"What did your parents say when you told them?"

"I didn't tell them. We got in a fight and that's when I ran."

"And you hung out here how long?"

"Maybe a week. Then I started to run out of food."

"How did you end up calling me?"

"Samuel's Mom didn't have a cell phone. She had this handwritten book with phone numbers in it. Next to every name and phone number she had little notes. Like 'PTA' or 'Bad driver.' Samuel showed it to me once, because she said some pretty raw stuff. Next to his old babysitter she wrote, 'Whore.' If she liked someone, she'd draw a flower."

"Was my name the only one without a note?"

"I'll show you." Jack pulled an address book out of his pocket. It reminded me of childhood, landlines and rec rooms and typewriters. I flipped through the alphabetical listings until I found my name.

"I see." We stared out at the water. Then we both burst out laughing.

"I figured I'd call you first."

"Yeah, a note that says, 'HOMOSEXUAL SINNER' in all caps would be my first pick, too."

"Also I liked your name. Sadie."

"It's not my real name. I picked it, just like you picked Jack."

"What was your old name?"

"My dead name? I don't like to talk about it."

Jack nodded. "Dead name. That's how I feel, too."

"Wait a second. So do your parents think you're Samuel? Do they think you were the kid in the ambulance? Why aren't they looking for you?" It just didn't make sense that his parents wouldn't be hanging around, looking for their kid, even if they were confused about who their kid actually was.

Jack was quiet.

"I mean, that wouldn't be the worst way to run away."

Jack shrugged. "Does it matter what I had to do to get here?"

"Yeah, I think it does."

"Why?"

"I need to know you didn't hurt someone on purpose. Just to get away. I mean—I need to know who I'm dealing with here."

"You're dealing with Jack. You know me, Sadie."

"I really need you to explain."

"Fine. My parents don't believe in the vaccine. They think the Democrats are using it to control peoples' minds and turn them against President Trump."

I rolled my eyes. "Go on."

"I told them I had vials of the vaccine in the freezer and I was going to inoculate them all in their sleep. That kids everywhere were going to inoculate their Republican, Trump-loving parents in the middle of the night."

"You're a genius."

"It worked. I scared them so much they left. They left me here and drove on home."

"And you haven't heard from them?"

Jack took his left shoe off, then his right. Dumped them upside down, shaking out sand. His eyes were red. He looked away from me. "I called my mom once. Said it was Jennifer. Said I wanted to come back home. She said, Jennifer who. She said, I don't know any Jennifers. She said she had a daughter before, but her daughter was dead."

A lightning strike of rage shot through my body. I realized then that you didn't need to feel maternal to be nurturing. You could just be angry as hell.

"Take me back to Seattle," Jack said. "Don't leave me here, Sadie."

It was already what I'd been thinking. I'd been preparing the words in my head. "I'd like to, Jack. But I have to ask my partner and my roommates. They're my family. We make decisions together, mostly."

"But they don't know me. They might not like me."

We walked back to the condo. I put my hand on Jack's shoulder. It felt like family was supposed to feel.

"Jack. It's going to be okay." I sat on the sofa and patted the cushion next to me. "I'm going to call everybody. I know they'll say yes. You'll see."

Jack slid closer as I started the Zoom call. Kate, Lina, and Richard appeared on screen, all sitting together, too. For the longest time everyone was quiet. Then Kate startled babbling, in that cute way that made me fall for her all over again, describing how they could decorate Jack's room.

"We have sort of a storage closet? But I could take a sun lamp and put it behind a screen so it's a fake window you can turn on and off. Or we could put up a screen in the dining room. We'll make something special for you, Jack. Someplace that feels like home."

"Do you like dogs, Jack?" Lina asked, as first one, then another dog face sniffed the screen.

Richard waved. "Hi Jack," he said. "We can't wait for you to join the family."

When I hung up, Jack and I just looked at each other. We smiled and kept smiling until we started laughing.

"Do you want half a burrito?" I asked.

"I think it looks kind of tired," and it did.

"Tell you what. I'll order pizza and pick up more ice cream and we can have a real celebration. You're gonna move to Seattle, Jack."

"What's it like there?"

"I'll tell you when I get back, okay?"

"Sounds good."

While I was driving, I thought about Alki Beach and Gas Works and the Ballard Locks. All the places we'd go, climbing hills where houses tilted precariously over the Sound, looking up at the sky through rain that never seemed to stop, but also never really started. The halfway place, green and restless. Home.

"You're gonna love it, Jack," I said to the dashboard. The pizza smelled so good, buckled into the passenger's side. A few more blocks and I pulled into the complex, rows of identical condos. I climbed the stairs and realized all the lights were on. The front door was unlocked; Jack's shoes and coat weren't in the closet. I saw the note on the table before I knew he was gone.

LOVE OF WAX

Lina didn't mean to have an affair. She wasn't that kind of person. Except, now she was.

"It's not dumping someone if you're married to them," her mother said. "It's called divorce, and it's what your father did to me. Goddamn asshole."

Lina held the phone away from her ear. She knew what was coming next.

"You should join a book club. Be an intellectual, for god's sake, Lina. We spent all that money on your college education for what? For you to be, what's it called again?"

"An esthetician," Lina muttered.

"Exactly. That thing you do with wax."

Lina listened through clenched teeth. Her mother didn't understand her love of waxing, her frustration with her husband, or her hatred of book clubs. Lina loved spreading hot wax over her clients' legs and armpits. She loved sugar paste and peels and lasers and manual lymphatic drainage. She loved scrubbing her clients' skin until bits sloughed off and she loved dunking hands in scented sudsy water and choosing the exact shade of polish to match the look they wanted. She loved thinking about beauty, both in relation to people and in relation to inanimate objects. She spent every weekend arranging, moving things around the house so that it felt different. Brendan never noticed. Pippa just purred and clawed the sofa indiscriminately.

Lina married Brendan because they went to the same gym and she was bored. She often flipped through dating apps while she slogged away on the stair climber. One day she noticed Brendan looking over her shoulder. He hurried away when she turned her head. After that she noticed that he stood as close to her as possible on the machines, without ever seeming creepy. A few weeks of this, and without ever speaking to him, without knowing his name, Lina decided she would marry him. Any other guy would've said something rude. Brendan was just waiting, as if he'd always been there. What Lina wanted was a man who would wait, who would be in her life but not expect too much from her.

When Lina told the story to her friends, she made it sound romantic. She described meeting Brendan at the gym with the elegance of a black-and-white film. Actually, romance had nothing to do with it. Lina was pragmatic. She wanted to be married because all her friends were getting married and doing things in couples. Some of her friends were even on their second marriages. And the babies. Babies, babies, babies. Lina didn't want a baby; that was one thing. Babies were expensive and it was hard to have a beautiful home when there were stinky diapers and spit up cloths everywhere. Having a cat was bad enough. Lina loved Pippa, but she drew the line on a creature that talked.

One day, while Lina was half-heartedly jostling along on the stair climber, she noticed Brendan standing beside her, matching her pace the way he usually did. She decided it was time.

"I'm Lina. What's your name?" Secretly she'd been calling him Lachlan. She'd always liked that name and hoped she was right.

"Brendan." He stopped moving and stumbled backwards off the machine.

Lina felt the first of many twinges of disappointment. Brendan was a good, solid name, but it wasn't Lachlan. Also, he was naturally clumsy. She was clumsy, too, which did not bode well.

"Are you married?" Lina thought she should get this one out of the way quickly.

Brendan looked surprised. "No."

"Do you want kids?"

"No." He paused. "I'd like to adopt a dog, though."

Lina was a cat person, so this was unwelcome, but Brendan's eyes were dark brown, and he was slightly taller. He wasn't married, didn't want kids, and was obviously crushed out. Lina had always hated dating. It felt so useless, such a waste of time. Spending money and weekends on someone who was just looking for something wrong with you so they could end it. Lina wondered if Brendan would be okay with her moving furniture around every time she felt restless, and if he respected her profession.

"I'm an esthetician." She spoke firmly. It wasn't a question.

Brendan stopped all pretense of climbing the imaginary stairs and wiped his forehead with a towel, even though he wasn't sweating. "That's cool. Skin is important. Skin keeps everything in."

Lina nodded. It was true. "Would you like," she hesitated, wondering if she could just ask him to get married, "to go out to lunch?"

"Sure." He looked relieved. "Right now?"

"I'll need to change first."

"Of course." Brendan was flustered, shyly looking at his feet. They walked together to the dressing rooms. "Well, see you back here in a bit."

After a lunch date, a dinner date, and sex, Lina asked Brendan to move in with her. She told him she needed a roommate (false) and that her cat hated dogs but had dog-like qualities (true).

Brendan agreed so calmly, so pleasantly that Lina assumed he, too, was ready for marriage. They were both just too rational and respectful to say so.

It was that easy, Lina told her friends. There were no big discussions about the meaning of relationships, no fights, no negotiations. They decided they were a couple and then they were. They ate dinner together, had sex twice a week, and took turns choosing which shows to watch. Eventually Brendan proposed, and they had a casual summer wedding with 50 guests, 9 of whom didn't show but still sent gifts.

✷

The marriage went on for several years.

✷

Then, at Brendan's stepsister's wedding, Lina stepped on someone's toe while reaching for a chocolate-covered strawberry at the dessert buffet.

"I'm sorry."

"Hi, Sorry. I'm Kate."

They shook hands. Lina laughed, and introduced herself. Until that moment, Lina had never considered that she might be attracted to women. Meeting Kate, however, Lina decided that she was now a lesbian.

"Let's dance," Kate said, putting her hands on Lina's waist.

"No one's dancing and there's not any music playing."

"Why should that stop us?"

Kate rocked Lina back and forth. It was the sexiest thing Lina had ever done. She caught Brendan's eye from across the room. He smiled and waved. He wasn't even jealous because he didn't understand that she, Lina, a mousy white woman in a pale yellow dress, was on fire for Kate, a mousy white woman wearing a rainbow bow tie and a dark blue suit.

While they danced, Lina noticed a woman with purple hair and a Cheshire smile staring at Kate. Their eyes met.

"Who's that?" Lina pointed her out to Kate.

"That's my partner, Sadie."

Lina felt crushed. Here she'd decided she was a lesbian and fallen in love at first sight, only to discover that her soon-to-be-wife-following-a-hasty-divorce-from-her-actual-husband was already in love.

"I'm sorry. I wouldn't have flirted with you if I'd known you were with someone."

"It's cool. We're poly. Sadie has a boyfriend." Kate spun Lina around. "Are you flirting with me? You might need to try harder."

Lina stepped back, still holding Kate's hands. She felt giddy, as if she'd walked into the illuminated pages of her favorite book. It was the life she wanted, without knowing it existed.

"Do you like dogs?"

Kate nodded. "Cats, too."

"I'm an esthetician."

"I'm a massage therapist."

They stared at each other, a look of mutual understanding for the seriousness of a job where a body lay naked under a sheet. Then they danced again, pressed close this time. After, they exchanged phone numbers. Lina watched Kate walk away, watched her kiss Sadie and put her arm around her waist. Sadie gave a little wave. It took Lina a minute to remember she had a husband.

While Brendan drove them home, Lina checked her text messages over and over, hoping Kate would text, set her new life in sync.

Brendan put one hand on her knee without taking his eyes off the road, the other hand carefully guiding the wheel. "You looked beautiful tonight. I'm so lucky, Lina."

Lina heard him through the static of television, as if she was watching a show about a woman who was leaving her husband. Already she was a character in another life. She imagined painting wax over their doors, their windows, and peeling it off to reveal the newness underneath.

Kate hadn't sent one text, but none of that mattered. Lina could see ahead and what she saw was Kate. Brendan's words filled the car, the slight pressure of his hand on her knee. She would wait to tell him. She would linger in the waiting, wondering what Kate would say, what life would happen to her next.

RAGE ANIMALS

I wanted to adopt an animal, but my landlord wouldn't let me.

"No pets," he said.

My landlord was white, with thin flat hair like mine. We looked like brother and sister, except he owned 20 apartments and I owned none. We weren't related. We just looked alike, the way white people did in my town. Actually, maybe we were related. We lived in Beau Bucket and my last name was Bucket and so was my landlord's. He owned four apartment buildings. I was in a six-plex, squashed in the middle, with no pets to make anything better.

"You could get a rage animal. There's a store downtown that sells them." He rubbed his chin. "I'd be fine with that, so long as you don't let it out."

All I knew was that I wanted a pet. If I couldn't have a cat or a dog, maybe I could have a rage animal. I just wasn't sure what kind of animal that was. Was it an actual animal, something with a complicated scientific name, too complicated to say? Was it a plushy? Was it a carnivorous plant?

The next day after work I stopped by the store. It didn't have a spoken name, just animal emojis painted over the door. A bell shook when I stepped inside. The room was empty, except for a large wooden counter with a cash register and rolls of paper.

Cora was sitting behind the desk with her feet propped up on the counter. I recognized her from Introduction to Social Media Marketing. She'd graduated the same year I had, but we hadn't hung out. I majored in Auto Mechanics and she dated in Tech.

The store had gleaming white walls and wood floors. The sign over the bathroom said *Water Closet* in old-fashioned script. Cora was taking selfies, smiling up at her phone, buttoning and unbuttoning the third button on her shirt. As I walked toward the counter she buttoned up and put her phone down.

"Hey Jack. What's going on?"

"My landlord said I couldn't have a pet, but he said a rage animal would be okay."

"A rage animal isn't a pet substitute. You have to know what you want, and you have to really want it."

I blushed. It was sexy, the way she said it, but was it supposed to be? I never understood things. Everything except the inside of cars was a confusing tangle of yarn I was trying to unknot with a ticking timer strapped to a bomb.

"Want to dance?" Cora walked over to a shelf behind the counter. She had a record player and a stack of records. She flipped through them, pulled one out of its sleeve: *Dusty in Memphis.* She held out her hand.

We danced around the room, goofy, then a little bit sexy. Then serious. We danced together and we danced apart. When I tried to pull her into me, she stepped back, laughing. Then she wrapped her arms around my waist and made me follow her.

After, we leaned against the counter to catch our breath. We drank water from mugs she kept by the sink.

Then I remembered. "What's a rage animal? Do I want one?"

Cora opened her arms and stepped forward, curtseying at the empty store. I looked around at the vacant shelves, the nothing and nothing and not one hollow word for sale.

"Am I my own rage animal? It's inside me, isn't it?" I hated the trick of it, the fake.

"Nope. Rage animals are totally real. You have to look harder. They're everywhere."

The store was empty. I didn't understand. I turned to face the door, then the wall, then something shifted. Out of the corner of my eye I caught a flicker of something moving. I stood very still. I waited and looked. Slowly their shapes became visible. Once I saw them clearly, I couldn't unsee. I sat down on the floor and stretched my legs out in front of me. The rage animal that chose me was butterscotch, with brown stripes and black spots.

I picked up my animal, my new companion. Walked over to Cora, who rubbed both hands into soft fur like she was giving a shampoo.

"What's her name?"

I handed her to Cora so I could think. I needed to pace and bob my head. My butterscotch companion gave a little squeak and looked at me panicked, so I had to think quickly.

"Velour Track Suit That Zips."

"That's her name? You can't call her that."

"You name her, then. Please give her back now."

Cora handed her back to me.

"Zippy," Cora said.

Zippy burrowed her fuzz-covered face into my neck.

OR

There's a bakery on every street corner, but Britt picked me to frost the cake.

"Of course she did," Richard shrugged. "She's my wife. You're my sister. Doesn't take a genius to do the math."

"I know it's hard for you to believe, but Britt likes me." It was true. We talked on the phone almost every day and texted first thing every morning. Sometimes, when she couldn't sleep, she'd send me selfies in the middle of the night.

"I'm glad you two are friends. Makes my life easier." Richard turned into the parking lot and pulled up in front of the doctor's office. "You gonna run in and get the thing?"

"We're early. My appointment's not for another twenty minutes."

He shrugged and turned on the radio.

I turned it off. "Which theme do you think she'd like better: satellites and stilettos or push-ups and pin-ups?"

"Shouldn't it be *or*? Satellites or stilettos."

"Don't start, Richard."

"Push-ups or pin-ups could go either way. Push-ups for strength or a push-up bra. Pin-up girls or pinned up against a wall."

"It's a serious question. I'm trying to do right by your bride."

"My wife."

I hated the way Richard said wife. Yes, technically Britt was his wife. I'd made their wedding cake three years ago. But he put the emphasis on *my*, like Britt was his and not herself. Like he bought some part of her when he gave her a ring.

Now here I was at the doctor's, finding out the sex of their baby. The doctor was supposed to write it down on a piece of paper and put it in an envelope to give to me today. Not to Richard or Britt. To me. I was the only person who'd know if their unborn child was a boy or a girl. Then I'd bake a cake for the baby shower. I'd use the inner layers of frosting to announce the baby's sex to the world. Britt and Richard would cut into the cake, two hands on one knife, everyone watching the blade. Pink or blue frosting would ooze out of the cake and the baby would move through the world on that wave.

When I first explained the idea of a gender reveal party to Britt, she thought it sounded stupid. But I had a way with her, sometimes more than Richard. I softened her into things. She and Richard met in law school, at a mock trial. They both wound up at the same big firm downtown.

"Why do you also need to be married?" I asked her once, after too many wine spritzers at a summer party.

She looked puzzled, as if she didn't have an answer. "He came next," she shrugged. "Marriage is good. It's a good life. You should try it sometime, Laura."

"No, thank you."

"C'mon. What about him?" She tilted her head toward some guy sitting with his legs wide apart, holding a beer can against his crotch.

Maybe I laughed then. Maybe I got up and left. Something was underneath everything she and I said, the thing Richard missed: about her, about me.

*

"Time's up," Richard nudged.

I hopped out of the car. "I'll just be a sec."

"For the sex."

"Ha. You're hilarious." I slammed the door to his truck. I'd wanted to do this all on my own, but my brother insisted on driving. Britt thought it was sweet. I thought it was selfish, the way Richard never wanted me to have time alone with Britt. I consoled myself thinking that at least I was the one who would open the envelope. I was the one tasked with making the cake, revealing their baby's sex to the world.

Inside the doctor's office I walked up to the receptionist, but she put her finger to her lips and motioned for me to sit back down. The office was filled with people in various stages of pregnancy. A few held babies in their arms.

"I'm just here for the gender reveal envelope," I whispered. "I'm not pregnant. I don't even like sex."

The receptionist pushed her glasses up the bridge of her nose. "I'm sorry. You'll need to take a seat. There's a line," sweeping her arm toward the waiting room.

I found a chair next to a stack of magazines and rummaged until I found *Entertainment Occasionally* and flipped through, gawking at celebrity gossip.

"I don't like sex, either." The woman beside me put her hand on my thigh. "My husband's done just like that and I'm bored to tears."

I turned to look at her. We stared at each other for a minute and I wanted to say something, but what? To comfort her? Tell her to get a divorce?

"It was a joke," lifting her hand from my leg. "But I'm sorry about your *husband*."

"Laura," the receptionist called, and I stood up, nauseous with guilt. The woman looked down and away, like someone had hit her.

The receptionist led me down an L-shaped hallway. "I'm Mary," she said, pointing to her name tag.

"Hi Mary." I wasn't sure if I was supposed to make small talk or if she was worried I was calling her "the receptionist" in my head, which I was. At the end of the L was a door. I reached for the handle, but Mary stepped ahead of me. "Make yourself at home," sweeping her hand across the room with the same gesture she'd used in the waiting room. Something about her felt so familiar. She was a robot I'd seen on TV. I stepped inside and she shut the door behind me.

It was a grieving room; I knew that right away. The colors, the furniture, soft music piped in. I sat down in a pale brown armchair. The walls were the gray of the lake when it rained in November, when geese flew in a great V from Canada. The music had notes of water and occasionally bird song. It wasn't really music; it was calming noise. It sounded like comfort food, like the chocolate I licked from my fingers late at night when Britt sent me selfies of herself in a sleeveless tank top and pajama bottoms, leaning casually against the bathroom wall in the house she shared with my brother, her husband.

If I thought too hard about the envelope, about the baby, I'd leak grief all over the pale brown chair.

After what felt like an hour the door opened and a man in a white coat walked into the room.

"Hi, I'm Dr. Bradfield." Holding out his hand, which I shook. His handshake was delicate and carefree. "I've got your gender reveal paperwork right here."

"Thanks," I reached for the envelope.

"Not so fast," he said, and I hated him for it. He pulled the envelope back, taunting me. "Do you understand that this is a unique situation?"

"Sure," I said, understanding not at all. Did he say this to everyone? Was he a religious fanatic, a creep, or just eccentric?

"I'll give you room to read the paperwork," and he walked to a corner of the room and stood facing the wall.

For a moment I wondered if Richard and Britt were playing a trick on me, if they were about to fling the door open and yell, "Surprise!" There'd be a cake with *Britt Loves Laura* written in yellow frosting. When I cut the cake, it would be hollow inside.

Instead I opened the envelope and pulled out several sheets of paper. I'd been expecting a sticky note that read *Boy* or *Girl* or maybe *One of each.* I hadn't expected a letter.

"Can I read this in the car? It's long."

Dr. Bradfield turned around. "Oh! Hi there. I'd forgotten you were in the room. Sure, do whatever you want. You're not my patient," and he walked out the door.

I made my way down the L-shaped hallway. It seemed to go on forever, more an E than an L, then a whole alphabet of turnings, rooms with doors, rooms with curtains, women moaning, babies crying. I couldn't find the waiting room. Finally I saw an *EXIT* sign. If I pushed on the door, would I trigger an alarm? But I was lost. But the building went on forever. I pressed my hip to the exit bar and stumbled outside.

I wasn't in the parking lot. It looked like the back or the side of the building. There were trees and a picnic table. Lining the road were three men and a woman, all holding signs that said *Baby killer!* and showed gory photos of what were supposed to be dead babies. I walked up to the woman.

"Lady, they don't do abortions here. They help women like my sister-in-law get pregnant."

She wrinkled her nose at me. "Are you a lesbian?" She stepped back, then pointed her sign at my stomach. "Get away from me! Stop! You're attacking me!"

No one did anything. The men kept facing the road, waving their *Baby killer!* signs at cars. I decided to ignore her, too. I walked over to the picnic table and sat down under a tree.

I took the letter out of the envelope and smoothed it out, print side down. I was scared to read it. What if Britt was sick? What if they'd found a tumor, a bullet, a hole inside her that never stopped, that bled and wept and imploded, and she was dying, and my life wouldn't have meaning anymore? What if the pages were blank?

I flipped over the letter. I started to read.

✳

It was getting dark. I was supposed to be inside twenty minutes, tops, and three hours had passed. I figured Richard would be gone, and I'd get a rideshare back to my place, but he was there, sleeping, seat pushed back, engine on, music humming. I knocked on the passenger door gently, then louder. It took a while for him to wake up.

"Laura? What happened? Is everything okay?"

I slid back in the seat and closed my eyes. "Everything's great. I've got a cake to bake."

✳

The next morning I needed to walk and think, so I borrowed my friend Quinn's dog Theo.

"More free time for me, bonus walk for Theo. Need anything from the store? I'm going today."

I shook my head. "Thanks for asking." I never needed anything from the store. I knew I was the kind of woman people tried to take care of, but in a bland way. No one pushed me up against their car and slid their hand under my shirt in broad daylight. No one drove across the country just to knock on my door. No one wept because I said I was leaving and they couldn't imagine life without me. I was just the kind of woman you knew would take good care of your dog, the kind of woman you'd buy coffee for if you were already on your way to the store.

Theo pulled me all the way to the park, a curve of sandy grass on the shore of the lake. We trotted through a pack of dog-like humans and made our way through trees to the secret beach, which looked out at the lake and jutted up against a golf course. Sometimes I watched men golfing just to remind myself of what I didn't need: a man in a pastel shirt and white pants, staring with fierce concentration at something other than me. The man was looking for something tamer than the lake, which was already pretty tame.

Geese flew above, honking. Shimmered a line across the lake and disappeared.

That was when I noticed the creature.

Too big for a dog, too small for a deer, it gazed unwavering across the golf course. I remembered a particularly frenzied exchange on the neighborhood app, warning everyone that a cougar and her cubs were roaming back yards and forest trails. The creature didn't shy away. It seemed to root, staring out at me and Theo. If it was a cougar, it was hunting, and it was a short leap or swim away.

I called to Theo, backing slowly away from the creature. When we reached the edge of the park, we ran non-stop until we got to Quinn's.

Panting, I knocked on the door. She made me tea while I described the creature.

"It was definitely a cougar. Theo was so brave! It was a close call."

Quinn handed me a mug of tea and we sat at her kitchen table, Theo asleep by our feet. "Are you sure it was a cougar?"

"Positive. Too muscular for a dog and too short for a deer."

"Did it look like this?" Quinn held up a photo on her phone.

"Exactly like that, whatever that is."

"It's a coyote. But did you notice anything special about the coyote on the golf course?"

"No, how could I? I didn't even know it was a coyote."

"Did it move?"

"Nope. Totally still. Just staring at us."

"Did its head move?"

"Now that I think of it, no."

"Of course not. Because it's plastic. The golf course sets out plastic coyotes to keep geese from landing on the green."

After that, I started walking Theo at the park on the regular. I told Quinn it was to get exercise, but really it was to gawk at the plastic zoo. Once she told me I started noticing coyotes everywhere around town. But it wasn't just coyotes. There were domesticated animals, too: plastic cats on front stoops, plastic dogs standing on guard in manicured yards.

✳

Something Britt didn't know about me: I knew exactly when an avocado was ripe. I bit the puckered skin and peeled the flesh with my fingers.

I knew she liked dark chocolate, even unsweetened, the kind meant for baking. I knew she had a half-wrapped bar in gold foil in a drawer in the kitchen that she was always fussing with, peeling back foil.

The letter went on forever.

It was a letter to me.

She was stuck. She didn't know how to stop lying to Richard: about their marriage, about the pregnancy she wasn't having.

There was no baby.

She said she loved me.

She said the reveal wasn't a boy or a girl but a feeling like flying. She wanted everything with me.

I think I always thought that if I heard the words, I'd know just what to say in return. That "I love you" follows "I love you," that even a plastic coyote needs a mate. But all I'd ever known was the choices other people made. Guns or glitter. Satellites or stilettos. Because I'd never been able to choose I stood in the hollow. It was a quiet place, a place for thinking.

I picked up a pen and began to write back.

THE LESBIANS WHO DID EVERYTHING RIGHT

The lesbians who did everything right lived next door, in a remodeled brick ranch with mid-century modern light fixtures. I couldn't see their furniture, but the lights glowed softly through cream-colored shades. Sometimes the femme stood outside with a trowel, gently poking native plants, surveying her domain. She wore cropped linen pants and a floppy straw sun hat over shoulder-length wheat-blonde hair. Her butch husband seemed to time her evening arrival with the same slant of sun fading over their driftwood-inspired fence. She stretched one long leg out of her truck and ran her right hand through her dreads before unloading thick metal toolboxes as if they were matchsticks. Their two adorable children boy-and-girled it down the moss-infused paving stone walkway and hugged her in tandem while the femme stood beaming in the doorway, all *Look at my husband, bitches.*

I spent too much time staring from my bathroom window while I was flossing, my finger purple with how long it took. I worked from home, clocking in on my laptop, keeping things running, keeping cameras in line. Occasionally I took breaks to do laundry and chat with my neighbor in 403. She was the opposite of the perfect queers. She wore bright blue clogs, purple scrubs, and hot pink lipstick. Her eyes had that genius look, although it might have been hypervigilance.

I knew she was squatting because she told me.

"You're new in 403," I said, making small talk while I crammed coffee grounds into the food waste bin at the curb.

"403 is for sale. I'm squatting," holding out her palm, orange rind peeled into a tight white crescent. "You can use the rind in kombucha. Probiotics are important to me."

"Makes sense."

She looked pleased that I agreed with her. "Name's Hearthstone, but I go by Alexis. What should I call you?"

"Dominique," I said, which was no longer true. Dominique was the name I used when I worked the phone sex lines. We were required to use fake names, even if our real names were sexy. Someone else was actually named Dominique, but since she couldn't use it, I thought I should.

"Have you ever thought about what makes a woman's name sound sexy? Ruth isn't an erotic name. Agree?"

I nodded.

"So what is it about Alexis or Dominique?"

I looked up at our building, boxy 1960's slate-gray stucco. I'd bought a studio here because I could afford it, unlike the new buildings spun like cotton candy, high rises blocking Seattle's sparse sun. I figured my building would stand up in an earthquake. It was still surrounded by houses, which I also liked, because my third floor unit got actual light.

"You own land, don't you? You're a landowner."

"Technically I don't own the land."

"Homeowner, then. Do you have any weed?"

We got high in her place, which was staged to look like mannequins lived there with fake plants for pets. The layout was slightly different, and the view was better than mine. I could see into the perfect lesbians' idyllic back yard from her living room. It was relaxing, like watching season one on repeat.

"They're perfect," I said, pointing at the window.

"I'm not gay like you."

"Not because they're gay. They just do everything right."

"You seem perfect, too. You floss."

"How do you know?"

"I go through peoples' trash."

Nothing much to say to that, so I nibbled another corner of the brownie we were sharing. "What happens if you eat the whole thing?"

She popped the rest into her mouth. "We're about to find out."

"What if you get sick? Do you have insurance?"

She laughed so hard she choked. I patted her on the back, then whacked her.

"Of course not," choking and laughing. "We don't get perks."

We looked at each other. It was weird how not gay she was. Usually I could get straight women to give me at least a glint, but her eyes gave off nothing.

"You're really straight, aren't you?"

"I sure am. Did you think I'd succumb to your charms?"

"No, it's just—"

"You did."

"No, it's just that most women give off sexual energy if you talk long enough."

"How would you feel if a man said that to you?"

"It's not the same thing. Oppression and stuff."

"Whatever. When I'm stoned all bodies seem gross."

Giggles erupted between us, as if we had given birth to a hilarious baby.

"It's so great that pot's legal now."

"You care about that? I see that you do." Her eyes got that glint then. "Okay, gay lady. If you had to sleep with one of the perfect lesbians, which would it be?"

"They're not my type. Too perfect."

"How would you describe your type?"

"My best friend Ella."

"Why don't you date her?"

"It wouldn't work. We're too different. She's nice."

"You seem nice, Dominique."

"My name's not Dominique."

"My name's not Alexis."

"I know. It's Hearthstone."

"My name's not Hearthstone. That's where I work."

"You work at Hearthstone?" I tried to picture her showing up for work in an assisted living facility, offering edibles to Grandma and Grandpa.

"Why do you think I can't afford rent? It's not because I don't have a job; it's because I do."

That made sense, stoned or not.

"You're in tech, aren't you?"

"Yeah, but not like that."

"Like what?"

"Not like rich."

"You own a place." She shrugged. "Look, it's not a big deal. I belong here as much as you do. As much as anyone," pointing in the direction of the perfect lesbians.

"What's your real name?"

"I can't tell you."

"Why not?"

"You might rat me out."

"But you said I was nice."

"That's what nice white ladies do."

"I'm not a racist."

"I didn't say you were racist. I just said I won't tell you my name."

"Then I won't tell you my real name."

We sulked in tandem. She broke first, laughing so hard I had to laugh, too.

"Fine," I said. "It's Jessie. And I'm not—"

"Whatever you say. That's on you to prove."

Footsteps stalled on the landing and the door key clicked.

"What do we do?" I whispered, frozen.

"This way." She grabbed my arm and we ran into the bedroom. For a split second I thought about all the wrong places this decision might go. But what was my alternative? She slid open the closet door and I followed her inside.

✳

The phone sex line was supposed to be retro, erotic in a playful way. We were supposed to tap into nostalgia for the 1960's, pretending we had landlines wrapped around our wrists while we were speaking, even occasionally pretending to get disconnected, as if someone pulled the cord out of the wall in a fit of passion. I took the job because I didn't have to show my face or my body. How bad, I thought, can voice work be? It turned out to be very bad. The job left ordinary words—"hand," "service," "please," "hungry"—laced with meanings I couldn't control. Every time I spoke to a stranger in the grocery store or at the post office, I felt as if my sentences contained little poisons, aerosols that lingered in the air long after I left the room.

✳

Not-Alexis and I stood in the closet, breathing each other's breath. We heard the tap-tap of heels and flex of shoes following. A confident voice talking about windows and sun.

"Is there another bedroom?" a soft voice asked.

"No. Just this one."

"The square footage seems off for one bedroom."

"Why hasn't this place sold?" A third voice, firm. "It's been listed for what, five months?"

"The previous owners passed away and there were issues with the will."

"Is everything cleared up now?" The soft voice, anxious.

There was a slight pause before the realtor said, "Nothing to worry about."

"We don't want any trouble. Everything needs to be perfect."

"It will be."

"Looks like a nice big closet."

Shoes tap-tapped and flexed toward our hiding place. Not-Alexis grabbed my arm. Suddenly I was somewhere else, like falling into a hole except out instead of down. The darkness of the closet receded. A light flipped on. We were in a room almost the size of my studio, facing a desk and a bed. There were two windows covered in pale curtains and a door on the opposite wall.

Not-Alexis touched my arm gently. "The secret door's here," pointing to the faintest seam in the wall. "You just press against the wall with your shoulder. It's not actually locked, just hidden unless you know where to look."

"How did you know?"

"I've lived here for years."

"You've been secretly living in this building how long?"

"It wasn't secret until recently. This room was made for me. It's my bedroom."

"Wait, where does the door go? Can we get out that way?"

"You know the bookshelf in the living room? The one filled with fake books and weird plastic knickknacks?"

"I sort of remember fake books and a vase."

"It's a bookcase door. Easy to get in and out of if you know where the latch is. I don't usually go through the closet. It used to be one big room until they made it my room."

"Who's *they?*"

"Rachel and Ted."

"Who is Rachel and who is Ted?"

"The previous owners."

"You knew them?"

"Yep."

"But they—"

"They died a few weeks apart. A year ago. I've been here the whole time."

"Did they know you lived in their closet?"

"We all lived here together. I mean, not in my bedroom. This place. We cooked dinner together. Watched TV."

"Were they your parents?"

"No. But we were a family."

"Chosen family."

"Exactly," she said. "I'm a nurse, but Hearthstone doesn't pay much. I take a lot of home care jobs on the side. At first it was just a few hours each week. Then Rachel fell and broke her hip. Ted needed help with his insulin. I started staying longer hours. They couldn't pay me more than they were already paying, so they let me live here and I saved on rent. We ate meals together, watched TV in the living room. They were both so smart. So funny. When I'd bring a boyfriend over they always called me their daughter. My bedroom was the laundry room, but who needs this much space for laundry? There's a stackable in the kitchen anyway."

"So this room, this hidden room is why the square footage is off on the listing."

She shrugged. "The realtor doesn't know. Whoever moves in will probably figure it out. But right now it works best to keep it private. I sleep here at night and stay here when there's a showing. It's safer this way."

I looked around. There were several photographs of an older couple. Watercolors of birds and wildflowers. Magnets from every state arranged like a map on the fridge.

"Have you been to every state?"

"Haven't you?"

I shook my head.

"Why not? Don't you want to know where you live? White people. You invade shit and then don't even visit."

The edge in her voice made me uncomfortable. It wasn't my fault; I wasn't like that. When male clients got agitated I always said the same sexy things to calm them down, but with straight women I never knew what to say. I tried changing the subject. "Do you paint?"

"I painted these. Ted was an artist. We'd paint in the kitchen while Rachel was writing. He showed me how to use pastels, then watercolors. We never got around to oils."

"Can I ask a question?"

"I think you just did."

"You don't have to be mean."

"Just spit it out."

The pot had worn off. We were both sad-eyed and tired.

"What was the dispute around the will?

"Me. I was the dispute. They left me this place, like I was their daughter. We were a family. For years. But they have a biological son. He never came to visit them. Never called or wrote or anything, just waited for them to die, and then challenged their will in court. Got a lawyer to argue they weren't of sound mind. Got a lawyer to argue I was just some Black girl out for their cash. He was white and good looking. Said the usual racist stuff about me."

"That's terrible."

"This is my place. I'm not actually squatting. They rewrote their will a year before they both passed. It's hell to listen to realtors trying to sell my own place out from under me while I hide in the closet. Rachel and Ted would be furious. I sort of feel helpless but mostly I'm scared. Once someone buys the place, where will I go?"

We sat down on the edge of the bed. She opened the curtains and the room filled with memories that weren't even mine.

✳

Not-Alexis told me story after story. She had a photo album, the old-fashioned kind, and a rotary phone that looked like it belonged in a museum.

"They didn't have cell phones. They used landlines. Can you imagine? Ted would take photos with his camera and I'd take the roll and get it developed down on Market Street. He was a photographer when he was younger. She was a reporter. That's how they met. They were covering the Vietnam War. He'd been married and divorced; that's where the son came in. The one who kicked me off their will."

"I wish I'd known them. By the time I bought my place—"

"I know what you're thinking, but they were still here. So was I. They just didn't leave their apartment. Back then they were all about conspiracies. It was a difficult phase. Later, you know, they sort of let go of all that. But there was this period where they were obsessed with conspiracies and I had just had to roll with it. Because I loved them and that's what you do."

"Conspiracies about what? Like the moon landing and stuff?"

"No, it was really depressing. They thought there would be this sickness. A pandemic.

That everyone would get sick at once."

"Like Ebola."

"Like that. But they thought it would happen in the middle of another conspiracy, like they had all these conspiracies layered on top of each other. It got hard to keep track. They were convinced— well, Ted was convinced, and he convinced Rachel who tried to convince me—that some rich white reality TV star would get elected president after Obama. The white dude would think he was a god and America would become a fascist police state."

"Whoa."

"I know, right?"

"That makes me sad. I mean, what a shame that no one learns about American government in school, right? Checks and balances and stuff. Like, the constitution and everything. I mean, there's nothing to worry about. This is America."

"They said a lot of Americans were arrogant and privileged and didn't get how quickly things could turn on a dime. They'd seen governments fall. They'd traveled around the world, taking pictures, writing for newspapers, and they said people here were complacent."

Not-Alexis stood up and opened a cabinet. It was filled with canned soup, boxes of latex gloves, and face masks. "Whatever happens to me, I'm keeping this stash. Might come in handy if I'm sleeping under the freeway." She held up a box of face masks. "You never know what you might need."

"You won't end up under the freeway."

"How do you know?"

"That's just silly."

"I mean it. How do you know?"

"I guess I don't."

"Well then, don't say things you don't mean."

I almost told her about the live cam then. How my life wasn't what she thought. How my life revolved around revealing everything to strangers while protecting my privacy just enough to keep myself safe.

Watching the perfect lesbians through my window was like my live cam, only it was free. I watched them while men watched me, and no one got what they wanted.

"They're gone for sure," Not-Alexis said.

"How do you know?"

"I have a camera in the bushes by the front entrance. It's for my own safety. Like a nanny cam but my place is the baby."

Everyone in Seattle had cameras for something. So many eyes. So many blank smiles.

We stumbled out of the closet. The light through the bedroom window hurt after all that dim. The realtor was gone, little card tossed on the kitchen counter, shades in the living room pulled down all the way.

I pulled up the shades and stared at the perfect lesbians' back yard. They were looking up in our direction. Pointing and squinting.

"It was them!" I felt so excited. "The perfect lesbians were the couple looking at your place."

"Great. Now I'm fucked."

"They're cool, though."

"Cool? What's cool about any of this? I'm going to get kicked out of my invisible illegal room by your dream couple so they can rent it out to some tech bro."

"No one's kicking you out."

"You don't understand how this works."

"I'll go down and talk to them."

"Talk to them? Are you nuts, Blondie?"

"Look, they have a beautiful house. They're beautiful people. They'll understand that you want to stay."

"Want to stay? I don't have anywhere else to go. I make ten dollars an hour emptying bedpans. I don't even get paid Seattle's minimum wage because Hearthstone's across the city limits. I can't afford to live here and I can't afford to leave."

Her anger was making me nervous.

"Calm down. We'll figure this out. We'll just tell them."

"Tell them what? That their future investment property has a squatter living in the closet? That the whole place belongs to her, but she got disinherited by someone's greedy, no-good son?"

"I'll tell them that they have to let you keep living here."

"Let me? I'm not beholden to them. They're not beholden to you. That's not the way the world works, Jessie. If you tell them about me, they'll call the cops."

"I can handle the cops. Let me do this for you." My mouth turned sour and bossy; I couldn't help it. It was this thing I'd always done, the thing that got me kicked off the cheerleading squad and bad grades in Chemistry, because Mr. Ford liked pretty girls and didn't need someone like me making faces every time he messed up his own experiments.

"I'm tired," Not-Alexis said. It wasn't a statement. It was a command.

✳

I left, taking the elevator back to my apartment the way I did sometimes even though it was only one floor down. I liked the sensation of being carried, cared for and escorted somewhere else.

For dinner I ate lentil stew from a microwavable bag. Half a box of frosted animal crackers. Then I flossed and streamed one of the cooking shows. The pastries were incredible, light and pale, towering toward the top of the perfect white tent.

✳

When I worked the phone sex lines, I got good at lying. Not white lies, but chunky lies, like a macaroni necklace I wore all the time. Lying was just part of the job. Making words into whatever someone else wanted them to mean. The first lie was always my name: "Dominique" sounded sexier than "Jessie." The lies after that were mostly about my age and my cup size.

After a few years I couldn't do phone work anymore. I couldn't take it. But by that point I had this giant gap in my LinkedIn profile. I'd gone from college to grad school to nothing for several years. I didn't know how to explain the gap. What was especially frustrating was that sex work was work, hard work, and I wanted credit. I wanted my skills at the top of my resume just like everybody else.

For a while I drove for the big rideshare companies. After that I got a job as a barista, which I liked. For the sunny side of a year I had health insurance and five paid sick days a year. Then the small coffee company I worked for got bought up by a coffee giant and my job didn't transfer. They just let me go.

The day I got laid off was the day I started my live cam. I was exhausted and worried I couldn't pay rent. I thought about going back to phone work—if a door was ever always open, that door sure was—but then I remembered my friend Mel, who'd switched to a live cam and made tons of money. The trick, she told me, was to find a niche that didn't require too much work.

"Take cake sitting. There's a lot of prep and cleanup involved. Plus you'll end up hating cake and who wants to hate cake?"

I had to agree.

Pacing around my basement apartment I tried to think of a fetish that would require very little effort on my part, low level nudity, and wouldn't reveal my face or my street. I made coffee. I made more coffee. Working for a coffee company meant I had lots of coffee in my freezer, spilling out of my shelves. Then it hit me: I'd make coffee with my top off and drink it while men watched. Men, maybe the odd occasional dyke, although I didn't want to get my hopes up. And so *Hot Cups* was born. It was so stupid and easy. I just had to be careful, every day, to make sure the camera was angled correctly. Once I accidently moved it slightly and realized everyone watching could see me brushing my teeth at the bathroom sink.

Weirdly, live cam was easier than phone sex. All I did was turn it on. Over time I realized that I had enough tech skills to add other cameras, other windows into peoples' lives. I didn't even have to put out an ad. I just recruited. Soon I had 54 women and 5 men working for me, drinking coffee with their tops off, holding their cups in their laps while they looked up at a camera and smiled or showed teeth.

∗

I decided it was time. Time to talk to the perfect lesbians. It took me a week to work up my nerve, to walk up to the door and knock like I meant it. The husband answered the door. She was so good looking that I felt a swoon down my spine. I'd lied to Not-Alexis about neither one being my type. The butch was definitely my type.

Also the femme. Also, maybe they were poly and would want a cute third to loosen things up.

"Hello," she said, looking amused or maybe completely uninterested.

"Hi, I live next door." I felt silly. "Up there. Not the top, just the third floor. But I can see you. I mean, into your yard. I mean— you're perfect. So is your wife. Your kids. Your whole family. I love midcentury furniture, too. I mean the lamps. I mean your fence and your paving stones."

Her expression didn't change.

"I'm not selling anything. I'm not with a church. I mean I'm gay too."

"What now?" She was blocking the door with her body. Her wife had stepped up behind her, but she was blocking the door and I realized she was scared. Scared of me.

"I'm not scary."

"I'm sorry," she said, beginning to shut the door.

That was when I might've taken things a little too far. I put my arm out, like shaking hands but more like blocking the door, and then we all just stood there, my arm trespassing, the perfect lesbians horrified by my inappropriate and possibly illegal arm sticking out in space.

Then the femme stepped into the doorway. "I know you," she said. "You're Ella's friend. You're Jessie."

"How do you know Ella?"

"We do Pilates together. I'm Laura."

"You're Laura?" The way Ella had described Laura-from-Pilates was so ordinary. Some married lady with kids who did Pilates twice a week.

"Ella talks about you all the time."

"You too!" I lied.

"This is my spouse, Britt."

"Nice to meet you, Jessie." Britt stepped back, vanishing into the house.

"Come in," Laura said.

And just like that, I was inside.

*

Laura motioned me into the living room I'd been staring at for years. It felt so strange to be in the bottom half of a room whose top half I knew by heart. Like kissing someone you'd only seen masked at a ball or in a conspiracy theorist's pandemic.

"So I have to ask you," Laura leaned forward, her tone intimate, "what do you think of your building?"

"My building. I love it! I mean I've only lived here three years, but my place gets great light and it's so convenient, shops and restaurants and—and—schools. And parks!"

Laura smiled. Up close her smile was different, less serene. There was some tight screw underneath. "I'll tell you a little secret. Britt and I went to a look at a place in your building the other day."

"Really?" I tried to sound astonished.

"We're looking at investment properties in the area. Building a nest egg. We thought it would be easier to manage rentals nearby. But I was wondering—just between you and me—is someone living in the unit?"

"It's not rented out. Just staged."

"I mean illegally."

I remembered Not-Alexis laughing at me for caring that pot was legal. I couldn't rat her out.

"We just wondered because we've seen the unit several times. We're concerned about—well, I'm concerned. Britt doesn't seem to care."

"I'm sure if someone was living there they would leave? When it sold?"

"Would they?" Laura looked at me then and I realized it wasn't a question. She was giving me instructions. I thought about Not-Alexis and how she'd gotten screwed over. I couldn't do something like that. I couldn't betray her. But then I thought about how somebody had to buy the place. And if it wasn't the perfect lesbians, it might be anyone. Anyone would surely be worse.

Laura folded her hands in her lap the way my mother taught me to fold my hands. Her hands were very white. Her hair had red undertones and I knew she'd been taught, as I was, to always wear sunscreen. It was about cancer, not getting any, but it was also the pale sheen of the whitest skin and how delicate she looked, her face almost not there.

"If someone was living there, and they just needed another place to go, would you have any suggestions?"

Laura's mouth did the same thing my mouth was did. That twist. It was like we were sister wives. I imagined eating dinner together, smiling with the kids as we passed plates of food around the long wooden table.

"They could go to an apartment that they paid for." Her tone was clipped. "They could go to a hotel. They could go to a hostel or a shelter. There are many places for people like that to go." She stood up. "I need to check on the kids. It was nice talking to you, Jessie. If you'd like to have good neighbors, think about what you might do to help. We'd love to share your building."

∗

Eventually I stopped doing live cam work and just took charge of other peoples' cameras. I needed more more money to buy a place. It was safer, too. No chance I'd be recognized. No chance I might slip, tilt the camera so someone could see a street sign, my name or address on a letter, anything they could place or plug into facial recognition or Google Earth or whatever people used to track down the person or thing they wanted to own.

Running the system meant I had all the cameras pulled up at once, mostly women, AFAB and transwomen and enby people who used the word woman tentatively. A few gay men. I stopped using coffee as a gimmick and let the work be what it was. The google search terms weren't refined, just woman, camera, live, nude. They didn't fuck onscreen. At first I admit I watched them, too. I felt terrible. They were paying me to manage the live feed and here I was, staring. So I stopped. I stopped looking at them like they were people. I focused my eyes on the tilt of the lens, on the clarity or blurriness of the image. I tried not to see the actual image, just shape and design.

I slipped up once. There was one camera, one feed I couldn't stop seeing. Her name was Victoria, and although I knew it wasn't really her name I thought of her as Tory. As mine. I watched her sleep and I watched her wake up and I watched her undress in front of the camera. She didn't know. I didn't do any harm. But then I just couldn't help myself. I slipped up. I had all the women's names and addresses to send them their checks and I mailed her a letter along with her check. I thought she might be gay, and she lived in Portland, driving distance, and she had a cat. I thought we had a lot in common. I didn't have a cat but wished I did. She had some of my favorite authors on the nightstand by her bed, and striped sheets, which I've always loved. I don't know if she got the note, but she never wrote back, and then just quit. I had to move all of Tory's viewers over to Violet. They looked sort of alike.

∗

The next day I walked to the market for bread. I bought two loaves, thinking I'd give one to Not-Alexis, but on my way back home I paused in front of the perfect lesbians' perfect house. I opened the gate and walked carefully up the paved path. Then I knocked.

Laura answered with her finger against her mouth. "The kids are napping," she whispered. "Come in."

We sat in the kitchen. Laura put on water for tea. We talked in quiet voices while the kids slept. Laura told me how she and Britt met at a straight friend's wedding, and how giving birth to their kids had made Britt softer, a better partner. Britt was a lawyer specializing in Elder Law. She did pro bono work repairing things for seniors who were aging in place.

"She's not as angry as she used to be when we were younger. Of course, racism will always be an issue. Britt's had to deal with so much. But parenting really brings out her light-hearted side. And I love being a homemaker." Laura smiled a tight-lipped smile. "What do you do, Jessie? Ella didn't say."

Phone sex, leading to live nude cams, leading to a job managing live nude cams.

"I'm in tech." No one ever pressed me. No one ever wanted to know more. Tech was subterranean worlds paved with one word.

Laura leaned in. "I should probably confess."

It was hot, how she said it. The image of the two of them eating each other out on some massive blonde wood bed flashed through my mind. I bit my lower lip, twisted it around.

"This isn't our first investment. We have several other rentals in the neighborhood. We're cultivating a curated portfolio."

"Could she live in one of your other places?"

"Excuse me?"

"I was thinking—I have a friend who needs a place."

"We run credit and background checks."

"It's just—you might want to help her. Helping her might help you, too."

That was how I outed Not-Alexis to Laura.

Laura listened while I explained about the room in the closet, about how Not-Alexis had nowhere to go. "The thing is, she's not really a squatter. The place actually belongs to her. There was a dispute with the will. The owners left the whole condo to her. But their son did something terrible. I mean, maybe you know. Britt probably sees these things all the time. It's, like, racism. How it makes things unequal. I mean, you could help."

Laura was silent. Their huge clock ticked its hands across the wall. The wooden floor held its satiny stain.

"Thank you for your honesty, Jessie."

"Of course." Telling the truth felt sexy, like watching her mouth say my name.

"I already knew about the squatter. I just wanted to see if I could trust you. It's great to have a neighbor we can trust."

All the times I'd watched them through the window and then touched myself. All the times I'd come with my fingers inside, imagining them watching me on their bed in this house.

"Yes," I said. And then again, "Yes."

✳

I tried to tell Not-Alexis that they knew. I knocked, and when that didn't work, I slid a note under her door and then another. Nothing. Finally I stood outside in the middle of the day, in front of her live cam. I played a game of charades, gesturing toward the perfect lesbians' house, gesturing toward her apartment, then toward me. I did this over and over again while people at the bus stop across the street pretended not to watch.

Then I gave up. Went inside and checked my live stream feed. I had thirty-two women open at once, each earning money for keeping the live stream live, each sending some of that money to me.

Later that week a big *Sold* sign went up on the *For Sale* sign in the window of the lobby. I texted Laura and she texted back right away: *We're your neighbors now!* She followed it up with a yellow heart emoji. I had to look that up: yellow for friendship. I felt giddy, and giddier when she called me a week later to ask if I'd like to walk through the apartment with her.

"I have to take some photos for the property management company. We're hoping to rent it out as soon as we redo the floors."

I buzzed Laura into the building as if she was a friend coming over for coffee.

"Would you like to see my place?" I'd rehearsed the question over and over, smiling into my mirror until I got it just right.

"Maybe another time? Britt really needs me to pick up some dry cleaning and the kids are at my Mom's. But thank you! It's so sweet of you to offer."

We stood outside 403 while she fumbled with her keys. Suddenly I realized that Not-Alexis would know it was me, would recognize my voice. She'd hear me casually chatting with Laura. She might think I'd sold her out, when all I'd done was tell the truth to someone who deserved it. It wasn't fair that Not-Alexis expected me to keep her secret. Still, I thought I should probably stay quiet. I figured I'd let Laura do most of the talking.

The staging was gone, and the condo felt hollow, as if I'd unwrapped an orange to find nothing but rind. Laura was oddly quiet, just studying the walls, occasionally taking measurements with the tape measure app on her phone, snapping photos of the most utilitarian features: light switches, appliances, the bathroom sink.

As she stepped into the bedroom I began to feel sick. If I said anything, Not-Alexis would hear me. It was strange knowing something Laura didn't know about her place. I imagined how it would feel to finally tell her, once Not-Alexis was actually gone and Laura and Britt were redoing the floors.

"Do you hear something?" Laura asked.

I shook my head.

Laura walked toward the closet. Then I heard it: the faintest sound of a telephone ringing.

"That sounds like an old-fashioned landline. Like there's a phone in the closet."

"Oh, that's just 303 downstairs. Sometimes sound travels through the vents."

Laura looked confused.

"I'm in 302 so I hear them a lot. They like old-fashioned things, landlines and train sets and—and—whiskey. And pulp novels. I can hear those, too. They read from them. Out loud. While they're drinking whiskey. I mean like it's performance art but they're alone."

None of this was true, but Laura chose to believe me. She didn't open the closet door. The ringing stopped, and we talked about nothing. In the kitchen while Laura took photos of tile, I noticed there was a tiny watercolor propped against the sink: the size of a postcard, an image of a telephone cord tangled like a snake. I slipped the postcard in the pocket of my sweater. The back was signed, a name I couldn't decipher.

✳

A few days later I knocked on Not-Alexis's door again. I thought maybe we could sit together in her hidden bedroom and plot out what to do. It had been almost a week since I'd talked to Laura. They'd given me two weeks to warn her.

This time, my knock creaked open the door. I knocked again. Nothing. I tiptoed inside. The apartment felt dead, like the heartbeat of its appliances had stopped mid-pulse. In the bedroom, I stood for a moment remembering heels tapping on the floor while I breathed Not-Alexis's breath in our hiding place. I looked out the window and saw Laura's garden. Then I opened the closet door.

Inside it was pitch dark; I had to feel my way to the panel. But there was no door, just an opening. I walked right into the secret room and turned on the light. It was smaller than I'd remembered. No bed, no desk. Just a washer and dryer and an empty plastic laundry bin.

As I was leaving I noticed something on top of the washer. It was the box of facemasks Not-Alexis had showed me. There was a note taped to the top: *You never know what you might need.* But the box was empty.

THE NEXT STORY

This time, the story writes itself.

You're in the grocery store and someone passes by with their cart. You stare into each other's eyes above your masks and feel desire, or you stare into each other's eyes and feel sadness. Whichever way it goes is the story you write. One of you follows the other into the parking lot and offers up a phone number or a list of names. Maybe the vaccine is ready. Maybe the vaccine has been distributed, free of charge, at-risk populations first, and so you kiss. This time, the story leads you to its minor characters all on its own. Someone turns their car into the lot just as you're kissing, just as the electric connection that will haunt you forever sparks inside your heart. Someone jumps out of their car, shouts, "That's my wife!" Let's give this minor character a name. Let's call them Rough Henry. Let's call them Bartender, Make That A Double. Let's call them Spider Saved While Taking A Shower. Let's not call them again.

Let them go.

Minor character, all that.

You Are Here.

You're in the grocery store and someone passes by with their cart. You recognize each other from seventh grade. She held your head in the toilet while the other girls kicked you because you were gay or fat or smart or all of the above.

Let's give the girl holding your head in the toilet a name. Let's call her Work Husband. Let's call her In-flight Magazine. Let's call her Collect. Let's give her a shiny new Charlie's Angels lunch box filled with sandwiches and notes from Mom. Let's say she breaks one of the metal soap dispensers when the tussle breaks out, when she twists your arm behind your back and pushes you down to your knees while gritty pink cherry-scented soap drips from the broken soap dispenser.

Let's turn on all four hand dryers at once.

Let's flush all the toilets, including the one holding a girl in ill-matched plaid, standing on the seat, sneakers untied, arms pressed against the stall. The door to Plaid's stall is broken. All the doors to all the stalls are broken. Plaid knows she's next, and she is.

You turn a corner with your cart and produce unfolds around you, rainbow. Glistening apples; hard yellow bananas; fuzzy kiwi; piles of carrots with green tulle tops. You've got a knife in your apron pocket and you're cutting cardboard boxes. Sometimes you peel an orange and wrap the curl around your wrist. You draw a clock's face on the peel. Starting now it's noon forever.

Sometimes the door opens and Plot rushes in, scarf around her neck, matte red lipstick. Sometimes she's running away, sometimes chasing. When her scarf slips off, you pick it up.

Every impulse tells you to tie her scarf into a bow. Every impulse tells you to make her beautiful, hold up a mirror and let her adjust her lipstick, her pose. Every impulse you have is wrong, so you hold the scarf over your head until it becomes an umbrella. It isn't raining, but when cops push back on all of you with shields and barricades, when they pepper spray faces, you hold up your umbrella and three of you huddle beneath. Facial recognition follows you. Helicopters buzz overhead and you sleep at a friend's house. The city smells like smoke and surveillance. When you leave, your friend says, "Text me when you get home, so I know you're alive." Apartment animals wait for their people as sirens scissor the city to scars. You walk until you're lost because new buildings pop up on streets you thought you knew. Now you are the minor character. The city moves through you as if your name doesn't matter.

PLASTIC FRIENDS

We needed to hide a key in the new house. The hardware store had three designs of hide-a-key: a fake rock, a working but unreliable semi-fake outdoor thermometer, and a fake water sprinkler. The rock looked the most fake and the water sprinkler looked like a gun. That left the working but unreliable semi-fake outdoor thermometer.

"Let's put the hide-a-key in the shed and bury the door to the shed in concrete," I said.

Patience was your best quality as you explained to me why this wouldn't work.

In the end we hung the working but unreliable semi-fake outdoor thermometer next to the front door because it matched the trim. However, neither one of us remembered to hide our key inside. When we got locked out a few weeks later you boosted me up to the fence. From there I climbed onto the garage and then the roof, where I lowered myself through an open window.

Before I let you in through the front door, I stood in the kitchen alone. Climbing onto the roof and through the window had changed me. I was older now, and wiser. You stood outside on the front stoop and I knew you were older and wiser, too. Now, I thought, we would change our names. We would get matching tattoos. We would plant hydrangeas.

But when I opened the door, you were driving away in a vintage car with *Just Married* soaped onto the windows, streamers and cans trailing the bumper. The woman in the passenger seat looked familiar. As you rounded the corner I realized she was our neighbor. She'd left her key in our thermometer, just in case you got locked out.

HOW I TRIUMPHED OVER PRETZEL'S DOMINION
AND BECAME A NATURAL LEADER

Before you left me for our next-door neighbor, we had many dogs together. Sometimes we counted ten, sometimes twelve. Once I was sure I counted thirteen, but you pointed out that the smallest one looked completely different from different angles and could easily be mistaken for another dog.

At night we slept on our bed in a pile of dogs.

I was not the leader.

You wanted to be the leader, but you weren't the leader, either.

The leader was the second smallest dog, Pretzel.

Later I wondered if this was where I went wrong.

In an effort to become more of a leader, I ordered a box of dog training books online. The books arrived one by one, each in a bigger box than the last. The final book arrived in a refrigerator box.

"I didn't order a refrigerator," I told the Amazon delivery person.

They just shrugged. They had 412 other deliveries to make that day and had to pee in a jar in the back of their truck.

Inside the giant box was my book, wrapped in yards of packing plastic.

Before I could displace Pretzel as pack leader, I needed to read my dog training books. Before I could read my dog training books, I needed a bookcase.

I went to the furniture store in my small town. I was looking for a bookcase, but the store was full of recliners.

Some of the recliners were overstuffed. Some had blue plaid upholstery. Some reclined all the way and some just tilted back.

The row of rocking recliners was inhabited by ghosts. The ghosts rocked back and forth as if they had nothing else to do with their time.

"What if I want to try out one of the rockers?" I asked the salesperson, whose name was Shelly.

Shelly nodded, as if she'd been asked this question before. "If you ask politely, any one of our ghosts will gladly give you a chance to try one of our rocking recliners. Also, all rocking recliners are on sale right now."

I didn't want to displace a ghost, but I also wanted to experience the rocking recliners for myself. I tiptoed up to the friendliest looking ghost, a headless body in a floral housedress, knitting a scarf.

"May I try your rocking recliner?" I asked the ghost. As an afterthought, "Thank you for considering my request."

The headless ghost stood up and brushed out the folds of their floral housedress. "Sure. If I can try your head."

It seemed fair. I'd never taken my head off before, but it turned out to be easy. While I rocked I thought about how it felt to be on someone else's body. My eyes looked at my body, rocking.

For the first time since you'd left me, I felt content.

I felt confident.

I felt like a natural leader.

The furniture store was filled with dining room sets.

Every dining room set had a baby. Every baby had a highchair that matched the tall chairs. The babies were plastic, with little knitted caps. White babies with flat, anxious expressions painted on their faces.

I didn't want a dining room set or a plastic baby. I wanted a bookcase. But there were no bookcases, only rows of tables with matching chairs.

All the tables without food made me hungry. I sat down at a long rectangular wooden table in an armless chair with an upright back. The chair was uncomfortable. After a while I made eye contact with the plastic baby, who looked uncomfortable, too.

"I'm really hungry," I said to no one.

It seemed inappropriate to sit next to a baby and not interact, so I stood up and untangled its legs from the contortions of the highchair.

The baby smelled amazing.

Almonds and salt. Vanilla, cinnamon, and chocolate.

Its arms stretched out to me or maybe it was trying to get away.

Was it marzipan or whatever gummy worms were made of, I wondered.

I poked its foot and pulled off its small striped sock.

Stale diseased air blew through the AC.

The babies I never had showed up on our doorstep. I was taking a shower, singing to myself against the water drowning the plastic curtain. You answered the knock, which couldn't have come from the babies, since they were swaddled and arranged head-to-toe in a large bassinette.

When I was dressed I walked into the living room and there you were, on the couch, with five babies lined up in a row. You'd turned the coffee table on its side and pressed it against the couch so the babies wouldn't roll off.

While I stood guard over the babies you rummaged through the fridge and came back with a Diet Coke.

"The Times just had an article about how Diet Coke addiction is real."

"I read that, too. They didn't say it was real, they said it might be real."

"Should we be feeding Diet Coke to babies, though?"

"Diet Coke isn't for the babies. It's for me."

You sat back down among the babies. All five were swaddled in the same sort of white cotton blanket. I picked up one of the babies and sat down beside you. The baby didn't cry or move.

"Honey, I think this baby is plastic."

"Of course it's plastic. Did you think it was real?"

The couch was uncomfortable with so many plastic babies, so we put them in a pile on top of each other. It was your turn to pick a show. You liked upbeat, predictable comedies and I liked Scandinavian crimes dramas with neurodivergent AFAB detectives. Usually we ended up watching compromise shows, things we could both be distracted by but would never love.

"What if we put the babies on the floor and wrote dialogue for them? They could have their own show."

You didn't say no or yes, just lifted each baby up and put it on the floor in front of the TV. Then you started humming.

"Is that the theme song?"

You nodded. You were making it up as you went along.

ME.ME.

You snapped a photo of me holding a plastic baby and posted it on Facebook.

In the photo, the baby and I had the same unflattering expression. The photo fit the many horrors of the moment.

A few of your friends liked it.

Then one of your friends reposted the photo. One of their friends reposted your post. By evening the picture was circulating all over the internet.

I wasn't on Facebook, so I didn't know.

You knew, though. You knew and didn't tell me. When we woke up the next morning, you drank the cup of coffee I brought you. You kissed me and I climbed on top of you, but my phone wouldn't stop pinging. The sound echoed in our bedroom. I thought someone had died. Instead my friends wanted me to know that the internet had taken one of my expressions hostage. That part of me belonged to the internet now. I was a meme about a tragic time and how it etches itself into a face.

But I was holding our baby.

But I was looking at you.

I bought a new phone.

When it was time to transfer everything from my old phone to my new phone, the guy behind the counter pulled a cord out of a box.

"Do I have permission to stick this in your ear?"

"Sure."

The guy stuck one end of the cord into my new phone and the other end of the cord into my ear. It was softer than an ear bud and fit perfectly.

"You might feel a slight whirring," he said. "Like wind."

I waited but couldn't feel anything. Still it was exciting, what new technology could do.

I stood while everything from my head went into my new phone, all that data bypassing the cloud.

Ten minutes passed. Twenty minutes. My right leg twitched a little from standing so still.

After almost half an hour the door to the store opened. A woman carrying two coffees walked up to the counter. "Got you one," she said to the guy.

Then she noticed me and stopped, staring. "Mitchell?"

He looked away.

"Mitchell!"

"I was bored."

She groaned. Walked over to me and yanked the cord out of my ear. "You can't transfer data from your head to your phone."

We both looked at Mitchell.

"It was an experiment," he shrugged.

The woman turned to me. In a voice so polite it was violent, she explained that she would be setting up my new phone and could answer any questions I had about the new system.

"I liked it."

"Excuse me?" she said.

"I liked the experiment. I think we should do it. I think it might work."

Mitchell jumped up and down, little jumps, like hiccups.

I turned my ear toward him. He handed me the ear bud. This time it felt even softer and shut out sounds around me. I closed my eyes, willing my brain to send every message, every photo, every password through the wire. My playlist echoed in my head on an endless loop.

TESTING

At work I took a personality test. It was considered a perk. Everyone shared their results online, splintering into subgroups, like liking like. At first people posted affirmations and anecdotes; then the mood shifted. Finger pointing turned into name calling and grievances.

My test results were blank. I had no personality. No one left hearts but no one criticized me, either.

At night I began to dream differently, neon colors and mazes, an elaborate bright sameness. I remembered seeing flamingos when I was a child. All that hot pink made my eyes tired.

At my retirement party, the theme was no gifts. They came wrapped in nothing, my name written on air. I'd long ago stopped showing up for work. Still the party mouths echoed, small bites of soft food.

At the gym we used the women's dressing room together. Sometimes when we used the dressing room together, white women looked at you in a particular way. Their faces contorted, not with envy or desire, but with violence.

The contortions of their faces had to do with men. They believed that you were a man and they believed that men were violent. Since they believed that men were violent, and that you were a man, they looked at you in a violent way.

When we were together and this happened, I was reminded that it also happened when we were not together. Also, I was reminded that it did not happen to me.

Sometimes you said nothing. Sometimes you left. Sometimes you turned your back and sometimes you took off your shirt.

I said nothing because the women didn't look at me, except occasionally to affirm with their eyes that you were violent. When they tried to affirm your violence to me, I gave them their violence back in the form of silence.

The women who believed that men were violent and that you were a man and therefore violent also slept with the violent men. The violent men they slept with were sometimes violent and sometimes not violent at all. They called these men "good men."

You were not a good man. They wanted your body to go away, to the identical room next door, where you were not welcome, either.

Sometimes when I was in the dressing room with the violent white women, I wondered who I was. If you were a bad man, was I a good man? If they were women, was I something else? If they were white and I was white and you were white, were we one body? If men were violent and women were violent, who was nonviolent? Was I looking with violence at someone else?

At night, when we'd left the violence of the dressing room, we ate dinner together. We cut our food with knives and forks. We moved together in the small kitchen. Outside, under the dry grass, invisible, trees shared information through a network of roots.

The dogs kept multiplying. The plastic babies kept multiplying.

You took off your shirt. You put your shirt back on.

Your tattoos were raised ink I came to know by touch: first a circle, then a star. First my fingers, then my mouth.

You with a needle. You with a razor. You talking with that frat boy neighbor.

On TikTok, nurses wept after 12 hour shifts.

5,993 Mississippi students tested positive in two weeks.

You ironed your shirts. You changed your name.

We tried to watch The L Word reboot, but their timing was wrong.

While I was trying to love you, there were many things you couldn't eat.

Some of the things you couldn't eat were common things and some were uncommon. For example, you could eat me, and I was uncommon, but you could not eat bread, which was common in the country where we still lived, in spite of everything that had been done to us.

Some of the things you couldn't eat were things I chose not to eat, and some were things that gave me pleasure.

You told me to keep a box filled with things that gave me pleasure that you couldn't eat. You said you'd never open the box, not even to look.

Years later, while you were away and I was alone, I realized I had never touched the box. It had become invisible, the way an urn becomes a vase.

When I opened the box, which I had never touched, I found a key.

The key was worn, but its teeth were sharp. I held it in my palm and studied the stain.

Now, because you've read so many of these stories, you want to know about the door.

Was the door invisible to me until I found the key?

Was the door there all along, locked in plain sight?

You want to know the sound the key made in the lock, the red inside, the slick.

You want to know about the meat.

One day I came home, and the babies were gone.

"I gave them away," you shrugged. "They were just plastic."

While I was out walking the dogs, I noticed babies in every window. When I asked you if they were our babies, you said no.

"So it's a coincidence that everyone is decorating with plastic babies now?"

"Barn doors and babies. It's the new thing."

The next day our neighbor was watering his flowers. "Bet you're glad to get rid of those babies," he said, spraying a sunflower in the face.

"Yeah, for sure."

"When I saw the box full of babies, I thought, whoa. I didn't take a baby, but I took the sign. Hope that's okay." He held up a big cardboard sign decorated with baby spiders and baby hedgehogs and baby jackalopes that said *Free Babies pls take one*

That night I asked you about my conversation with our neighbor. You listened attentively. Your face was completely blank.

"Bet I can make you forget about babies."

But because I had sung to them, because I had covered their painted eyes with my thumbs, because I had named them, I never did.

You wanted to be on lesbian TikTok.

I did not.

It was our first fight.

You filmed it for lesbian TikTok.

"Absolutely do not post that," I said. But we looked so good, you in a tank top and me with my sleeves rolled up, both of us in jeans and boots but different jeans and boots.

On lesbian TikTok there were words for everything, all the nuances of sex and design.

We did our little dances. I scratched the line of hair on your neck.

"How is this different," I asked, but you were outside, filming yourself leaning against a tree, catching the light at just the right angle. You were chopping wood, even though we didn't have a fireplace. You put a towel over your head and pretended you were me, taking hours applying my makeup before we went out on a date.

"Babe, I don't wear makeup. Babe, we don't go on dates; we stay inside and talk about ways we might die. Babe, can I have my towel back."

But there were two of you now, the one holding the camera and the one being filmed. It was getting hard to talk to you; you had so many fans. You needed to answer their comments, make little jokes about me with a towel on my head, how long it took me to find my mascara.

I went for a walk. The wildfire smoke was visible in orange streaks across the sky. Somewhere a group of people rushed toward a door in desperation. The door wouldn't stay open for long; they knew. They pushed and pushed. A child slipped from her father's arms. The father would not make it through the door and the door would close and the sound of the plane taking off would never stop, orange blur in the sky a knife across my skin. But I was just another American on film.

Sometimes we both needed to Zoom at once. You were convinced it wasn't possible.

"Why not try," I said, thinking of things that actually seemed impossible, like someday retiring from my job or doing hot yoga in a face mask or getting Afghans who helped U.S. forces airlifted safely out of Afghanistan.

"Okay."

"Is that 'okay' or 'ok,' because I can't see letters when you talk."

"O-K-A-Y."

"Okay."

You put on your bicycle helmet. You packed snacks. You went into your office and shut the door.

"ONE!" You shouted. "TWO! THREE!"

I clicked on the bright blue link. A page opened onscreen. It was not a page, but a door. Its doorknob pulsed. I touched the doorknob and a hole appeared on my laptop. I climbed through.

"You were right," I shouted from the faraway planet I'd somehow arrived in. The planet had a gray sofa, a brown desk, and a bookcase with a picture of your mother and brother. The planet was an office. The office was yours.

"Are you in my office?" I shouted.

You didn't answer, but I could hear your voice across the hall. You sounded like me. I looked down at my feet. I was wearing your shoes, made from recycled tires. My feet were your feet, meaning not my feet at all. I touched my face, which felt like your face, which I touched often.

Zoom was open on your computer. I waved at the screen and people waved back. I felt the sadness in your body move through your chest, your arms. I felt my own sadness radiating from across the hall. I remembered your snacks and opened a bar of dried fruit. Then the sound of a door opening, a knock, your name in my mouth.

Sometimes I didn't know what I was.

Sometimes I liked not knowing and sometimes not knowing felt lonely. Everyone else seemed to know what they were. Everyone else knew what they were and so they knew which door to open. Not knowing which door to open meant not knowing where I was in the first place, but also where I might be when I opened the door.

Every time I opened a door I found myself in a windowless room facing yet another door.

Other people opened doors all day. They said, "paint swatch," "hedge fund," "miniature pony."

When I was younger, people liked to tell me that one day I'd stop opening doors, either because there would be no more doors to open or because a dog sits when you give them a cookie.

Sometimes I looked in the mirror to see if I might catch a glimpse of what I was if I pretended I was a stranger. But I was never a stranger to myself, which was why I kept opening door after door.

When you looked in the mirror, you saw a door. You were never in the same room, either.

Sometimes we looked at each other and sometimes we looked away.

You bought a hat.

You got your hair cut.

You got two full sleeves of tattoos.

I stayed the same. I changed on the inside. But inside was a place, and I shared it with you.

Sometimes you felt familiar and sometimes you felt like a stranger. When we were both familiar, we touched in a particular way. When one of us was familiar and the other a stranger, we touched in different ways. When both of us were strangers, we touched in particular ways that felt familiar but not familiar together.

Other people had touched me. Other people had touched you, too.

Our curtains let in light and the outline of trees outside our window. Behind our house, our neighbors' yard was full of dog crates and dog pens, but no dog.

I thought the dog might be invisible.

I also thought the dog might be dead.

It was impossible to imagine our dogs dead. I didn't want to, not now, not ever. But it was not impossible to imagine someone else touching your body or you touching someone else. The idea that a body would move through space coming into contact with only one other body seemed unlikely. It was more troublesome to discover, for example, that I had accidentally eaten the tiny oval sticker on an apple or that I had left my sneakers outside in the rain.

Every time I touched someone new I experienced my body in a different way and therefore couldn't compare the experience. It was like before and after receiving the vaccine. After my first shot I sat in purgatory, which was a school cafeteria. Everyone waited 15 minutes to leave the room. I stared at the white tape on my left arm. There was only an intensity of feeling, the hot release of after, hummingbird pinprick of a wound beneath gauze.

We decided it was time to talk about the difficult thing.

The difficult thing didn't have a shape or a name. It was a thing that didn't exist before us but now existed between us. The difficult thing between us existed because of us. Because there was an us, there was the difficult thing. Before us the difficult thing did not exist and we did not exist, either.

Because the difficult thing didn't have a name and only existed between us, because of us, we had never talked about it before. We had talked about other difficult things with other people, but we did not exist then, and neither did the difficult thing.

Before we could talk about the difficult thing, we decided to do the easy thing we did very well. The easy thing between us existed because of us, and not before us, just like the difficult thing, except it was easy.

Sometimes before, with other people, the difficult thing was the easy thing and the easy thing was difficult. Sometimes there were only difficult things and sometimes the other people were strangers.

It was difficult to talk about the difficult thing, which made it more difficult, although the difficult thing itself did not involve talking.

It was difficult to talk about the easy thing, but the easy thing did not involve talking, which made it easy.

It was easy to talk about most things, but not the difficult thing or the easy thing, which made talking about most things easy.

Sometimes we watched TV. Watching TV was a way not to talk about the difficult thing or the easy thing, but to think about what existed between us because of us. It was easy to watch TV and talk about stories that existed outside us. We were inside, with a story between us. We sat on the sofa watching TV.

We moved boxes into the house by the river.

At night we could hear the river and also the train. During the day when we walked along the alley that was 6th Street, we could hear the freeway. The freeway sounded like a car coming up behind us. Sometimes it was a car and then we pulled the dogs into the bushes.

Our neighbors planted flowers in plastic pots along the back of their fence. Through the pots and the flowers and the fence we could see their chickens in a wooden hutch.

I spoke to the chickens and also to cats.

I spoke to the river and also the train.

You spoke to me or people far away when you had earbuds on.

The city surrounded us with lights and night noises.

The YMCA shuttered and decayed. A dog trainer used the brown grass for search and rescue rehearsals.

The bagel shop never opened. There were signs for a bagel shop and then it was empty.

At night you laughed at the stories I made up about the dogs. One dog was a milliner, another an opera singer, and a third had a secret love several cities away.

In this way we survived as the world closed in, as we no longer spoke to others, as we learned the names of the dead. In this way we waited for the names to reach us.

Every night we unfolded the paper with the long list of names. We knew to read the names aloud. We knew some day one of our names would be spoken and The Remainder would set the paper on fire.

You didn't know what the ending was. I didn't know, either. We knew what the beginning was because we made it together, but although we would make the ending together, we didn't know what it was.

The beginning was the same for both of us, but we spoke of the beginning as if it was different. For you the beginning was uninterrupted, but for me there was an interruption and therefore two beginnings.

We knew other things, for example other endings and beginnings and interruptions with other people. We knew that sometimes endings felt right and sometimes endings felt painful. We knew that death was an ending, and eventually the ending, but although death was the ending, it might not be this ending.

We knew that the dogs would suffer most from the ending, as the dogs had been happiest since the beginning.

The dogs had formed a pack from the beginning. Pack order was apparent to everyone. They trotted around the house in a line, eating and drinking and sleeping in the order they had chosen as their beginning.

The dogs filled the bed at night, rehearsing the ending.

We tried giving them treats to sleep on the floor, but they ate the treats and jumped back on the bed.

We slept hugging opposite sides of the bed. We had sex on the sofa or in the shower, which was hot, but sometimes at night I woke with one leg off the bed and one leg crushed beneath the barrel chest and hot breath of a sleeping dog.

Once I woke to find you asleep on the floor. The dogs oozed to fill my spot and there was no more room, just fur and floppy ears and teeth.

I took two pillows from the bed and lay down beside you. I put one pillow under your head and lay my head on the other pillow. You shifted toward me in your sleep. Above us the sound of dogs breathing and twitching and scrabbling in their dreams sounded like the train that rumbled down the hill. I knew I would fall asleep without interruption and wake up to a new beginning.

RECENT AND SELECTED TITLES FROM TUPELO PRESS

Made in United States
North Haven, CT
01 September 2023

40954755R00093